本书为2016年北方民族大学一般科研项目"文化'走出去'语境下宁夏乡土小说中文化信息的英译策略研究"(项目编号:2016WYKY04)的最终研究成果

Selected Contemporary Ningxia Works Translated into English

英译
宁夏当代作家作品选

Selected Contemporary Ningxia Works
Translated into English

吴坤 译

黄河出版传媒集团
宁夏人民出版社

图书在版编目(CIP)数据

英译宁夏当代作家作品选 / 吴坤译. — 银川:宁夏人民出版社,2017.12
ISBN 978-7-227-06860-0

Ⅰ.①英… Ⅱ.①吴… Ⅲ.①中国文学—当代文学—作品综合集—英文 Ⅳ.①I217.1

中国版本图书馆CIP数据核字(2017)第330279号

英译宁夏当代作家作品选　　　　　　　　　吴　坤　译

责任编辑　赵学佳
责任校对　闫金萍
封面设计　魏　佳
责任印制　肖　艳

黄河出版传媒集团
宁夏人民出版社 出版发行

出 版 人	王杨宝
地　　址	宁夏银川市北京东路139号出版大厦(750001)
网　　址	http://www.nxpph.com　　http://www.yrpubm.com
网上书店	http://shop126547358.taobao.com　http://www.hh-book.com
电子信箱	nxrmcbs@126.com　　renminshe@yrpubm.com
邮购电话	0951-5019391　5052104
经　　销	全国新华书店
印刷装订	宁夏凤鸣彩印广告有限公司
印刷委托书号	(宁)0008156

开　本	787mm×1092mm　1/32
印　张	5.625　字　数　200千字
版　次	2017年12月第1版
印　次	2017年12月第1次印刷
书　号	ISBN 978-7-227-06860-0
定　价	32.00元

版权所有　侵权必究

前　言

在漫漫的历史长河中，宁夏将古老深邃的黄河文化、浓郁粗犷的边塞文化、包容创新的移民文化以及特色鲜明的回族文化集于一身，成为一片文学创作的福地。作为对外宣传的窗口和宁夏文化的名片，宁夏文学取得了丰硕的成果。然而，宁夏优秀作品的译介工作步伐滞后，对其翻译中遇到的问题也未能引起足够的重视，这在某种程度上会影响中国文化传播和中外交流质量的提高。国人应该加强对外宣传，重视对外翻译。文学翻译是文化交流的一条重要途径。文学作品植根于现实生活，承载着一个国家、地区和民族的风俗、情感、思想和精神，最能体现其文化的精髓，是与其他国家、地区和民族进行交流的纽带，也能为有效沟通和共同发展架起一座桥梁。

宁夏乡土小说是中国文学的重要组成部分，是西北乡土小说的缩影。黄沙厚土孕育的宁夏作家以故乡为背景描写乡村生活，带有浓厚的乡土气息和地方色彩，笔触细腻，或恬静安详，或苦难悲壮，具有持久的感染力和生命力。这些乡土气息浓厚的作品中含有大量文化信息，涉及语言、物质、社会、生态和民族等方面，具体包括习语、俗语、口语、服饰、饮食、建筑、习俗等。作品中带有地方特色的文化信息应该在目标语中得到推介和传播,从而使更多对中国文化和文学感兴趣的外国朋友更好地认识宁夏、了解中国。合理的文化信息翻译策略和有意识的文化阐释对避免文化误读和冲突、传达深层的文化意蕴具有十分重要的意义,既要能向译语读者传递异域风情,还要考虑到翻译目的和读者接受度等问题,以达到文化传真,促进真正意义上的文化交流。

  本书为2016年北方民族大学一般科研项目"文化'走出去'语境下宁夏乡土小说中文化信息的英译策略研究"(项目编号:2016WYKY04)的最终研究成果。该研究以若干宁夏作家的代表作为翻译对象和分析文本,探讨其文化信息的翻译策略,期待能为翻译工作者及爱好者在此类文本的文化信息处理方面提供一些帮助,为进一步推进宁夏文化产品"走出去"贡献一份力量,为拓展中外文化交流的空间提供助力。

  由于译者水平有限,不妥之处,恳请读者朋友们不吝指正。

吴 坤

于北方民族大学外国语学院

2017年12月1日

# CONTENTS
目 录

《吉祥如意》 …………………………………… 1
  导　读 …………………………………… 1
  译　文 …………………………………… 4

《换水》 ………………………………………… 27
  导　读 …………………………………… 27
  译　文 …………………………………… 29

《赛麦娘的春天》 ……………………………… 55
  导　读 …………………………………… 55
  译　文 …………………………………… 57

《生命的节日》《夏日原野上的追赶》 ………… 88
  导　读 …………………………………… 88
  译　文 …………………………………… 90

《宁夏回族文化图史》(节选) ………………… 102
  导　读 …………………………………… 102

1

译　文 …………………………………… 104

后　记 …………………………………… 174

《吉祥如意》

导　读

关于作者

　　郭文斌，宁夏西吉县人，现任宁夏作家协会主席、银川市文联主席、《黄河文学》主编；为中国作家协会全国委员会委员，宁夏大学、宁夏师范学院客座教授；全国宣传文化系统"四个一批"人才，享受国务院政府特殊津贴，被宁夏党委、政府授予"塞上英才"称号。其作品涉及诗歌、散文和小说等体裁。黄沙厚土为他提供了丰富的写作素材，赋予了他不竭的创作灵感。著有畅销书《寻找安详》《农历》等十余部；有中华书局版精装八卷本《郭文斌精选集》行世。长篇小说《农历》获"第八届茅盾文学奖"提名，在最后一轮投票中名列第七；短篇小说《吉祥如意》先后获"人民文学奖""小说选刊奖""鲁迅文学奖"；短篇小说《冬至》获"北京文学奖"；散文《永远的堡子》获"冰心散文奖"。曾任中央电视台八集大型纪录片《中国年俗》、百集大型纪录片《记住乡愁》文字统筹；提出安详生活观、安全阅读观、底线出版观、祝福性文学观，并受邀到中央电视台等单位和北大、清华等高校及多省市演讲，受到欢迎。

郭文斌的小说语言笔触细腻，简洁凝练，自然流畅。他善于用简单的词汇表达丰富的意义。著名评论家张陵说："郭文斌用艺术的手段使西部的生存严峻性变成了一种诗一样的东西，他把小说写得值得玩味的地方很多，他小说的风格非常安静，这种安静在乡土文学中形成了一种独特的风格。"他的小说常常以儿童的视角或人性的视角来观察和感受乡土的坚硬与柔软，寓情于景，情景交融。诗化风格和精神诉求是郭文斌作品中非常宝贵的两种品质。

关于作品

《吉祥如意》2006年发表于《人民文学》，之后被《小说选刊》《小说月报》等国内多家知名刊物转载，先后获得"人民文学奖""小说月刊奖""鲁迅文学奖"，其中，"鲁迅文学奖"是与"茅盾文学奖"齐名的代表中国文坛最高荣誉的文学大奖。评委会对该小说给予了这样的评价："以优美隽永的笔调描述乡村的优美隽永，净化着我们日益浮躁不安的心灵。"著名评论家雷达说："没想到还有这么美、这么纯粹、这么含蓄、这么隽永、这么润物无声的小说。他的小说在理论上的概括可能不容易，但是你可以被陶醉。"

《吉祥如意》以温润平实的笔调塑造了五月和六月这两个人

物特征鲜明的儿童形象，他们的纯真和美好很能打动人心，小说深厚的文化背景是中国的传统佳节——端午节。小说通过两个孩子上山采艾前后发生的故事将一幕幕静谧和谐的乡村生活图景展现于读者面前，对于插柳枝、摆供果、祭祀、绑花绳、采香料、缝香包等节庆民俗和温馨美好的家庭生活的描写使作品具有了一种至真至纯的诗意和深邃厚重的文化意蕴。

宁夏是一块文学创作的福地，宁夏文学一度被称为是"西海固"的文学。其中，小说创作尤其突出。短篇小说《吉祥如意》就是代表作之一，具有乡土小说的鲜明特征。黄沙厚土孕育的宁夏作家以故乡为背景描写乡村生活，带有浓厚的乡土气息和地方色彩，表达了对故土的复杂情感。小说以平实细腻的笔调描绘出一幅幅乡村生活的画卷，恬静安详，纯净美好，具有强大的吸引力和生命力。小说具有独特的艺术特色：乡土风情的描绘、对美好生活的向往和追求，以及人性视角和儿童视角的运用等。这部作品既继承了文学传统，又追赶了时代潮流，在守护与创新之间达成了统一。小说语言朴实无华，洗练含蓄，细腻自然，仿佛是一曲乡野小调、一幅风俗年画或是一首文化诗歌。小说字里行间透露着作者热爱自然、返璞归真的精神诉求和美好期盼，它不仅具有唯美的文学性，还积淀着深厚的文化底蕴，这些主要体现在小说中使用的民间口语、方言、俗语、习语和民谣之中。

译　文

Bliss in Mugworts

Guo Wenbin

  Hit by a stream of aroma, May woke up. Mother uncovering the lid of the earthen pot in the corner of the kang (a heatable brick bed in North China), such wonderful aromas struck May's nostrils. June awoke, too. Their eyes open, a basin of steaming sweet fermented grains stood before them. With a blue-blossom porcelain bowl in the left hand, and a wooden spatula in the right hand, Mother said, "Look! It rose perfectly like our good days." May looked at June, and June looked at May. Sights encountering, they shared the joy at the good news. "Let me have a taste and see if it's true or not." May said to Mother, sticking out his tongue. "Not yet. After being enshrined, the food can be eaten on the Duanwu Festival （also called the Duanyang Festival or the Dragon Boat Festival）." Mother responded. All of a sudden, May and June rushed out of their quilts.

  It was before broad daylight that they got to the yard. Father was inserting the willow branches on the doorframe of the principal

《吉祥如意》

room when May and June regretted getting up so late. They went out of the gate, only to find willow branches inserted on the door of each household. This immersed people in the vitality of the whole alley. May and June ran to the end of the alley, and then back in a swift way. The long alley was suffused with the scents of willow branches as well as something indefinable. When standing at this end, they could gain a bare view of that one due to the heavy fog. However, the very effect accounted for the mysterious flavor of the Duanwu Festival in the hearts of May and June. When running to and fro, June felt countless secrets passing by with the sound of cracks; when stopping, they clearly saw the secrets swaggering amid the interlaced willow branches. On their second arrival at the end of the alley, June asked, "Sister, do you feel something?" "What?" May asked. "It's hard to say, but I felt it," June responded. "Isn't it the fog?" May wondered. June shook his head and felt disappointed because what his sister felt was far from what he did. "Willow branches, or what else?" May wondered. June shook his head again. May said, "I see. It is 'beauty'." June was amazed at his sister's uttering such a word, which hung on the lips as usual. But, beyond his expectation, his sister put the word into use on this very occasion, making him develop a sense of respect. He said to himself, "Why can't I find the word?" Later on, he sensed that it was natural for him not to come up with it, for the word never completely revealed what he felt. In other words, "beauty" was just a small fraction of something he felt.

When they came back from the gate, Father and Mother has set the altar in the yard; when they finished washing their faces, Mother had brought sweet fermented grains and flower –like steamed buns to the altar, followed by fresh pears and Chinese dates. In the misty night, there was a mysterious flavor as if innumerable legendary figures had waited to enjoy the delicious food before them in private places.

Having lit a stick of incense towards the heaven and offered rice wine on the ground, Father said with tremendous solemnity,

"Mugwort leaves smell sweet, scents pervading the court. Peach branches are inserted on the door; yellow wheats are overlooked outside the door. Here comes Duanyang. There goes Duanyang. Everywhere is Duanyang. Mugwort leaves smell sweet, scents pervading the court. Peach branches are inserted on the door; yellow wheats are overlooked outside the door. Here comes Jixiang (Auspiciousness). There goes Jixiang. Everywhere is Jixiang."

May and June had no idea what Father said next, nor did they remember it. Having finished reading it, Father led them in making kowtows. June didn't know whom they made kowtows to and wanted to ask Father. But Father's pious looks kept him from going ahead. June believed such a feeling of kneeling down to kowtow seemed fantastic. The ground was wet after rain, so the knees and forehead felt cool and fresh when touching it, as if a burst of electricity ran through the bones.

  Mother took the offerings back to the principal room, saying, "Grab a bite, and hurry up to pluck the mugwort in the hill." Mother got a small bowl of sweet fermented grains to each one and some steamed buns. Then, she split it into half along the yellow line of the middle, into another half along the red line of the middle, and finally along the green line. Mother gave May and June a small piece respectively, which they two treasured too much to eat it while holding it in the hand. How could people be hardhearted enough to eat such nice-looking steamed buns? But Mother said, "It is a rule that people must have some offerings before climbing to the hill." "Why?" asked May. "A rule! You must get to the bottom of it?" June said, "I just want to get it." Mother replied, "Offerings blessed by legendary figures are able to ward off evils." June added, "Really?" Mother replied, "Certainly, it is true." June added, "If so, we should have our meals enshrined every day." Mother agreed, "Ok, it was the case while your grandma was alive."

  Sweet grains were fermented by hulless oats, giving forth an intoxicating scent. Unlike the ordinary steamed buns, flower-like steamed buns were made of dry flour, with eggs and edible vegetable oil mixed. Then, Father pressed it one hundred times with the rolling pin, and Mother rolled it one hundred times by hand. After being softened in the basin for one night, the dough could be baked in a pan with slow fire. They could get it only once each year. It tasted soft and pliable, sweet and slightly salty. How could it be taken at one swallow?

Next, Mother tied up colorful strings for them, telling that snakes would stay away from them. June asked, "Why?" Mother answered, "Snakes fear colorful strings." June felt as if the wrist that had been tied up with colorful strings was filled with a powerful army, so they would no longer get cold feet. After that, Mother inserted a willow branch into each one's pocket. Such kind of all-out armed feeling could be responsible for June's spontaneous sense of mission.

May and June were walking in the fog of the Duanwu Festival. Now and then, June took out the colorful string on his wrist and had a look. June wore a three-colored string, partly concealed and partly revealed in the misty night, making people feel it was not just a wrist. What was it? He had no idea at that moment. June wanted to consult his sister May, but when seeing her, June thoroughly forgot about it. His sister was playing with her sachet when June almost collapsed because he left his own under the pillow. June was staring at the sachet in May's hand, with stars in his eyes. He couldn't help reaching out his hand for it. Pretty soon, May found her sachet missing. When May found it in June's hand, her face seemed to discharge flames with anger. Hurriedly raising the sachet before his nose, June smelled hard. May saw scents in flocks diving into June's nostrils. She was ticked off to reach for it. Unexpectedly, before she "seized", June returned the sachet to her. Staring at June's nostrils, May saw scents buzzing like bees in June's nostrils. Sure enough, the sachet never smelled as sweet as before. June's nostrils kept stretching, with just a tail of bee array left outside. May attempted to scold, but June's poor looks stopped her. At that time, the sachet was back to June again. June jumped back while raising the sachet before his nose to smell hard, his nostrils open wider like cave dwellings. May was so irritated that she rushed to June. However, as soon as her hand touched June's, the sachet was back to where it was.

"Hee-hee-hee!" May was amused by June. At this moment, June was just like a big nose, greedily opening or closing. A puff of compassion crept up to May. Anyway, rich water should be kept in our own field. Or it will do to let them have another smell. Thereupon, May passed the sachet on to June, but June refused. May asked, "Are you angry with me?" "No, scents have been in my belly." "Really?" asked May. "Sure." answered June. May added, "How do you know that?" June said, "I can see it." May said, "In the belly! What a waste!" June thought for a while, "That sounds reasonable. How could scents be unjustly put in a place filled with excrement? Or else, breathe it out." "It is a waste, too," said May.

"But I can breathe it out to your nose." June thrilled at his invention. May also believed it was a nice idea. Then, he opened his mouth wide and crouched down before June. With the strength of his belly, June squeezed the scents into his sister's nostrils little by little.

However, all of a sudden, June halted. He found his sister so charming when she closed her eyes, inhaling into her belly. The scents turned into a tongue, giving a kiss on May's forehead.

"Alas! A snake!" Sister jumped with fear. Looking around, June said, "No snake here!" Sister said, "Just now, a snake's tongue really gave me a lick on the forehead." June said, "Maybe, it is a snake fairy." "Did you see it?" asked May. June nodded. "What does the snake fairy look like?" asked May. June answered, "It is like a sachet." June answered. May had a look at the sachet in the hand, saying "It became an immortal. No wonder you like it so much."

Perfumes are elaborately selected when people make sachets. May and June specially went to a fair for perfumes. May said, "I feel like the most fragrant feasting your nose." "What's the good? I'm not your future husband." June replied. "Anyhow, feasting your nose is the top priority." They two headed for the fair with great joy.

Various perfumes were available in the fair. May kept smelling from one stall to another, from east to west, and then from west to east. She smelled through the whole street, but failed to make sure which one was the most fragrant and to buy. May was confused when she saw a girl older than her selected perfumes. So May's eyes were tailing after the girl's hand. May asked June, "She looks like a new bride, doesn't she?" Looking up and down, June said, "With the round butt and long plaits, she is so much like a new bride." May said, "If so, what she buys must be the most fragrant." Hence, May took the same one as the new bride did.

There was voice but no figures in the hill. Shrouded in the mist, May and June seemed not to have been born yet. June viewed the mist sweet-scented today. Somehow, June thought of Mother. He asked, "What do you think is Mother doing?" May thought for a while, "She may be making pastries." June said, "I see Mother sleeping." May replied, "Are you a clairvoyant? How can you see Mother sleeping?" "It's true. I can see her sleeping," June answered. "What is Father doing?" May asked. June answered, "He is also sleeping." "As we left, they indeed had gotten up. How could they sleep again?" said May. "Father seemed to be breathing the scents out to Mother," said June. May said, "Didn't Father carry off Mother's sachet, too?" "Perhaps..." answered June.

Suddenly, June said, "That's my sachet." With this, he ran back. May rushed to catch him in hand as if the eagle snapped at the chicken, saying "If you leave, what shall I do?" "I'll be right back when I get it," said June. Unfastening her sachet on the neck for June, May took a look at June and said, "I give mine to you." June was hesitating, motionless. May dressed June in person. Subsequently, June found, without any sachet on her chest, May became gloomy and poor-looking very soon, like a pole with flowers picked off. But he was reluctant to give it back to May. June thought, "Why do people love scents so much? Who on earth likes scents, human beings or noses?"

Later on, they were to select colorful strings. They found the street filled up with colorful strings. A lock here and another there, the street was kind of a big wrist. With two jiao clutched in each one's hand, May and June, like bees, smelled here and there, but were unwilling to spend them. Not until the fair was nearly over did they have to lay two jiao out. They were both holding five colorful strings, with beauty beyond words.

On the way back, June asked May, "whose new bride is the most pretty?" "It is yours," said May. "Take it seriously, please!" June was embarrassed. "How do you like it?" asked May. "It must be the street's bride," answered June. Surprised for a moment, May asked, "Why?" "He wore so many colorful strings around the big arm, sachets around the neck and perfumes all over the body. But for him, who else would be more worthy?" said June. Her eyes wide open like the brass gong, May moved closer to June's face and said with a smile, "How weird! How can you get such a wild idea? How can the street marry a new bride? If so, what kind of girl can deserve him?" "You can. I know you dream of it," said June. Hahaha, May burst into laughter. "Sister would be the happiest in the world," June said, "and I would be the brother-in-law of the street." May said, "Thus, we would have an unlimited supply of colorful strings and sachets."

The fog was still following them like a shadow. June's eyes exerted all their strength in an attempt to push the fog off, the cover of the fog ballooning. The rim of the cover was dotted with people. June said to his sister, "Look! They have already gone up the hill." May said, "Such early birds!" They two hastened the pace, breaking into a run.

On arriving at a ridge land, June said, "Isn't it mugwort?" May went over, and indeed found the mugwort with sparkling dew lying like quietly unblinking eyes. May had a look at the hilltop, saying "Why didn't they notice the mugwort?" June said, "They didn't look down at the feet." May asked, "Why not?" June answered, "They didn't think of it." Believing that June was right, May admiringly watched June and said, "How can you remember looking down at the feet?" June replied, "I thought of the hilltop, but somehow grasped a glimpse of the feet." "How unworthy tries people on the hill had!" said May. "I still want to go up the hill," said June. May asked, "Why? Isn't there mugwort?" June said, "I want to see people pick mugwort, and do it together." May said, "How about seeing Sister pick mugwort?" June answered, "You do it alone. It is so boring." May said, "But what shall we do if we run into a snake?"

June said, "We both tied the colorful strings and ate the enshrined flower-like steamed buns, didn't we?" May said, "Ok. Go ahead!" In fact, May wanted this, too. Why did people prefer going up the hilltop? The mugwort at the feet never stopped people from going up the hill.

When May was sewing the sachet, June made fun of her. "Oh, you must do it for your future husband." May chased to whip June. As June raced, he said, "Raise a hen to collect eggs, and marry an official to enter the county." But May always failed to catch June, which even surprised herself. As usual, she could easily catch him and pin him down to the ground. Later on, she got to know she really didn't mean to catch him. She just enjoyed chasing him. To be honest, she enjoyed June's yelling like that while running. It was so embarrassing. Running or halting, June stuck his butt up towards May and patted them by hand. May was turning shy. She pretended to be very angry, went back to the room and shut the door. No matter how hard June knocked at the door, May had no response. June had no choice but to keep apologizing and swearing. Then, May was wild with joy. She was fond of June's coaxing her. Formerly, each time June teased her, she always caught him, tweaked his ears and listened to him begging for mercy, as if a cat pounced on a rat. Now, she no longer liked that way. She felt extremely delighted and comfortable in hiding behind the door and waiting for June to coax her.

《吉祥如意》

Halfway up the hill, June couldn't keep up. June said, "Slow down a bit, ok? I was too tired to go any further." May looked back and smiled when she found the cover of the fog pierced with a cut, from which he saw the village lying there like a sachet. May's tongue rippled a kind of flavor — sweet fermented grains that Mother covered in the basin. May wanted to go home, but they hadn't got the mugwort — a year's auspicious omen. May urged June to hurry up. Instead, June simply squatted down.

"Whoops! A snake!" May suddenly shouted and ran away. June desperately ran after her. After a while, he overtook his sister, ran ahead and kept turning round to urge his sister. After running for a while, May lost control of her legs and plopped himself down halfway, laughing with a heavy breath. June turned round, and saw his sister sit there laughing. He gasped for breath, saying "Did you really see a snake?" May said, "Yes, I did." June asked, "What is a snake like?" "It is like you," said May. "It is like you," June said, "and you are a beauty snake." May said, "You said you can't walk any further, but how can you run faster than I?" Her words knifed June's heart open. "At that time, I hardly moved at all, but why did Sister's shout of 'snake' prompt me to race ahead of her?"

Whew! Snake! May sat motionless. June pretended to be running forth for a few steps. He turned around and saw Sister stand still. May said, "Mother once said that the snake is a spirit. As long as you don't hurt it, it won't bite you. Mother also says that the real serpent is in one's heart." June said, "Mother is talking nonsense. How can that be the case?" May said, "Mother also says that there are countless serpents in people's hearts. They each can throw dust in people's eyes, but even not find it themselves." June believed and then searched for it in his heart. After a long time, he still found nothing. In the end, he got to know the problem was not whether there was a snake or not, but that he had no idea where the heart was. He asked May, but it was also more than she could tell. Thus, a problem got its foothold in June's heart.

Mother said the sachet should be sewed in the shape of heart, with a three-color one hanging on the shoulder of the heart, and a five-color one on the tip of the heart. Generally speaking, each year, the new bride will ask someone to send sachets to her future husband's family before the wedding. Without a new bride, Mother and Sister had to make the sachets on their own. More or less, they felt sorry for it, but May could have a larger field of vision than June. May said, "It doesn't matter. Wasn't Mother a new bride in our family when she was young?" Therefore, June had a high opinion of May. June said, "Yeah, but whose new bride is she?" May roared with laughter. "Tell me!" June thought it over, but got nowhere. May said, "Father! You idiot! Certainly, Father's new bride, or who else?" June took a tumble. After listening to what May said, June suddenly felt something interesting between Father and Mother. Also, May had tried sewing two sachets.

Mother said, "An early sewer marries a good man." May was blushingly beating Mother with her fists. Mother added, "Men win by virtue of excellence, while women skills. Practice makes perfect." Hence, May practiced over and over again. She played with some cotton prints in her hands.

June forgot about it very soon. May really saw a snake. June could tell by the look on her face that Sister didn't cheat him this time. May, promptly and calmly, moved close to June, held him in her embrace and clutched his hands. Then, with her mouth pointing to the grass around them, June caught sight of a circle. They two discussed how to handle it by making gestures. June said, "Didn't we tie the fancy strings on the wrist? And didn't we eat the enshrined flower-like steamed buns? " May said, "Didn't Mother say that the snake won't hurt you as long as you never hurt it? " June said, "Didn't Mother say the real snake is in one's heart? Is the grass one's heart? Or is one's heart the grass? " May said, "In one'sheart is a poisonous snake. Maybe the one in sight is not poisonous." Just then, June felt a cold shiver all over the body, and then his belly began to burn up. May gave a glimpse of June, with a sign of snake on his face.

At this moment, the circle began to spin, sometimes very slowly and sometimes very fast. As they were sure that it got farther and farther, May and June smelled out a fragrance from the other side, one hundred times sweeter than that of sachets. It was not until the circle span where they believed safe that their sight encountered and then turned into water, streaming down along two places — one was the palm and the other June's trousers.

  Mother taught May how to use a needle and wear a thimble. For the first time, May took delight in pushing a needle into cloth with a thimble, piercing through cloth with a needle and stitching two pieces of cloth together. When May did some sewing, June flung himself on the kang and observed. How weird! Such a fine needle with an eye at the end could be threaded; following the lead of the needle, the thread could get through cloth; and pieces of cloth could be joined together; finally the "heart" in Mother's eyes was done. It was so interesting that June's fingers itched for a try. He asked Sister for a needle and thread, but Mother said, "A boy cannot use a needle." June asked why. Mother said, "A boy should hold a big needle." June asked, "What is it?" Mother said, "You'll learn it as you get older." June lay back on the kang, painting that big needle in his heart. How big? May wore Mother's thimble, which was a bit looser so that the needle unavoidably might slip off and prick May's flesh. Blood trickled and pain intensified. June hastened to dress her wound, while Mother remained unmoved. Mother said, "It is natural to shed some blood at the very beginning." June thought Mother was kind of indifferent. The needle in Mother's hand was more like her well-behaved adopted son. How could it be so obedient in Mother's hand?

They were approaching the hilltop. Never before did May and June get a wonderful feel of "all". Each one looked so cute. Even those who didn't deserve their attention at ordinary times were no exception. June reported his discovery to May. He whispered, "It seems that Disheng was not that odious." May replied in a low voice, "I feel the same way."

"Oh-oh-oh! You see June is like a new groom, isn't he?" said Disheng. Each one reacted, "You said it." Mangsheng said, "He is also taking a new bride along, his neck draped with bright red." June was somewhat shy and angry, but never flew into a rage. May said, "We've just seen a snake." Disheng said, "Really?" June said with pride, "Definitely yes!" Disheng said, "Don't brag. If you had really seen it, you would have peed your pants." June flamed up. May shielded June's disgrace, saying "It is you who pee your pants. If it were you, you might be scared to death." Disheng said, "If it were me, I would capture one and toast it for food." May said, "Don't brag all the time." Disheng replied, "If you are in doubt, capture one and let me show you." Baiyun said, "Shut up, please. My grandma said the snake is a spirit. It can hear anything and won't bite those who come from the good family." Disheng was at a loss. Baiyun answered, "It means the family who do good deed all their life, never eat meat or anything smelly." She added, "My grandma said that our village was once under the threat from a plague of snakes. Villagers tried every means to shut windows and doors tight, but snakes often crept into beds. Many people died from this plague. Only the Lis slept soundly every night, with the door open but snakes far away." June said, "Really?" Baiyun answered, "Absolutely true!" She stepped forward to pick up June's sachet.

"If you like it, take it." Such a generous response was even beyond June's own expectation. Baiyun astonishingly stared at June and felt as if the sun had risen in the west. June added, "I mean it." Baiyun said, "Really?" May gave a warning by having a few coughs, but June still insisted on and took it to Baiyun. Baiyun received it with hesitation. She seemed to wear a look of not deserving it or believing it true.

Disheng and Mangsheng clapped their hands, yelling "Baiyun is June's bride! Baiyun is June's bride!" At that time, the sun was rising up on the faces of June and Baiyun.

Father asked June to pound the perfumes. June picked up the stone pestle, only to find the perfumes mischievously jumping out. May said, "Let me try, please." Father replied, "Girls cannot do this." May asked why. Father said, "No reason." May pouted, "Why not let me do it?" Father gave June a demonstration and perfumes completely behaved themselves. June had another try, but failed again. May said, "Just a few perfumes have been screwed up by June." While collecting perfumes scattered on the floor back to the stone mortar, Father said, "At the beginning, this was the case for me. You have to explore and practice continu-

ously." Father's words boosted June's morale, perfumes jubilantly kicking and jumping. Step by step, perfumes behaved better and better. June was puzzled: when you exercise great care, they jump; when you cast caution to the wind, they stop. This keyed June up, as if a burst of electricity had run through his head, and someone had reached out to open a lot of windows in his heart. June found May full of envy on her face. June took pity on his sister. There were some things you could never do. Suddenly, June found the family divided into two parties: in one group were Father and him; while in the other were Mother and Sister. You see, Mother only taught his sister how to do needle work, while Father taught him how to use the pestle. Wasn't the pestle the big needle?

Sister helplessly watched him pounding perfumes, and eventually accepted the fact that it had nothing to do with her. Hence, she took cotton prints and started to sew the sachet. June's pestle up and down, sweet scents gradually pervaded the house.

The fog slowly lifted. People on the hill were increasingly clear, like a group of fishes emerging from the surface. June looked around, his delight knowing no bounds. Looking down the hill, June felt the village like a small tiger lounging there. Plumes of smoke were winding into the sky like a small tiger's whiskers. What a pity! They failed to enjoy the beauty, which was about to break people's hearts.

Unconsciously, the sun popped the head out of the eastern hilltop, like a sachet. June thought, "Not only did the hill spend the

Duanwu Festival, but it also wore the sachet." Everyone was lying on the ground to mow the mugwort as if hearing the order of the sun. June asked, "Why not pick the mugwort when the dew on them is dried up in the sun?" Sister answered, "While the sun just comes out, pick the mugwort, on which there are both the sun babies and the dew babies. The sun baby is the heaven's son, while the dew baby is the earth's daughter. With both in readiness, it can deserve auspiciousness." June felt it strange that Sister referred to the sun and dew as "babies", which Mother normally called them. Thus, June squatted down, took the cutter out of the basket and set about picking the mugwort. However, June stepped back. Drops of agate-like dew in brilliant shine seemed not just dewdrops but sons of the sun. June suddenly understood why Sister called the sun and dew as "babies". Just one cut would end several sun babies' lives. May said, "Why do you stare into space? Hurry up, while the dewdrops just wake up." June said, "I can't." May asked why. June said, "These dewdrops were too poor." May laughed, "I thought you felt the mugwort poor. You idiot! Even though you don't pick them, they will die when the sun comes up. This is their destiny. But they won't die because they will come back to life tomorrow morning." An admiration for Sister rose up in his heart. He didn't expect Sister to utter such a big truth.

June, however, found no way to start. Sister smiled again, "If you consider them pitiable, you can first give a good shake to keep them lying on the ground and sleeping slowly, and then start." June thought it a good idea and began to shake. This, however, cooled his ardor. In the eyes of June, such a shake proved that something beautiful could be gone so easily. He sensed the instability of beauty for the first time. What caused beauty to death was indeed his hand. Looking at his own hand, June felt it not simply a hand but something unfathomable. What was that? He couldn't figure it out for a time, but was not reconciled to it. "It's clearly my own hand, but why can't I see it through?" June began to doubt himself for the first time.

June started to pick the mugwort. Gradually, he distracted his attention from dewdrops and hands. Very soon, June immersed himself in another kind of happiness— picking. With the blade getting close to the ground and then cutting, mugwort tamely flung themselves into his hands, as if waiting so long for him. June remembered what Father said, "To pick mugwort is to pick bliss." Instantly, untold auspiciousness threw themselves into his arms, like a rising tide.

People all over the hill were picking bliss. How spectacular!

Mother taught May how to put perfumes in the sachet: sprinkle new cotton evenly with perfumes, pack the cotton into the sachet and then seal the sachet. Mother said, "Such a sachet will be both bulging and fragrant." June asked Mother, "Why is it bulging?" Mother smiled, "You have so many questions. Think it over yourself." June said, "What does Sister think of it?" May said, "It is not my question." June said, "My brother-in-law will prefer the bulging one." May beat June with shyness. Mother beamed from ear to ear. June said, "I suppose Disheng has a crush on my sister." Mother said, "Is that true? If Disheng becomes your brother-in-law, do you agree?" June replied, "No, I don't. He is not an official." Mother said, "Oh, when you grow up, study hard and try to be an official." June said, "Sure. When promoted to a position of leadership, I will marry Sister." May sheepishly pulled a quilt over her head. Mother gave a loud guffaw. June smiled, "What's the matter? Father always says that rich water should be kept in one's own field. Why will my sister marry the other man?" Mother said, "You have so much in the world to be confused about. Something in the world is precisely possessed by none other than outsiders. Giving brings about auspiciousness. So your grandma often says that give-and-take means that giving comes before taking. What you care about most should be given away first. The Emperor of Heaven creates this rule." June said, "The Emperor of Heaven is a dotard, isn't he?" Mother said, "He is absolutely not senile."

When the Empress of Earth took all her daughters back from mugwort, everyone called it a day. Standing up, June found Sister's Chinese-style coat like a curtain of falling water after being wet out by dewdrops. Sister took away the mugwort he picked, bundled them up with straw ropes and gave them back to him; then she scrubbed mud on the blade with grass. Exposed to the sunshine, the surface of the blade looked glittering. Sister having turned the blade, the dazzling light shed onto her face. Somehow, June thought Sister was like the mugwort at that moment. If she were really the mugwort, who would pick her? June was taken aback by this idea. If picked, wouldn't she die? However, everyone clearly regarded death as auspiciousness. Otherwise, why did so many people go into the hill to gather mugwort? June was in tangle again.

On the way back, June found that the mugwort others picked were a lot more than theirs. So he believed there were so few kids in their family. It occurred to June — why didn't Father and Mother go into the hill to gather the mugworts? He asked Sister. Sister responded, "Because they were not 'Tongnan Tongnv' (Chinese pinyin)." June asked, "Who are they?" Sister thought it over and replied, "Maybe, they are made of 'tong'(Chinese pinyin, here it refers to copper)." June thought it wrong, "They are clearly made of flesh, not copper." Then, he asked, "Why can't those who are not made of copper pick mugwort?" May said, "I have no clue. Father said so. You see. Those who gather mugworts on the hill are virgin boys or girls." A light breaking in upon him, June said, "I see. 'Tongnan Tongnv' refers to those who have never gotten married." Startled by June's opinion, May turned round and observed people in the back, finding it surely seemed that way. May read "waiting" on her younger brother's face, and expressed her appreciation with one move of "pushing into arms". Hence, June did feel proud of being a member of virgin boys and girls, and meanwhile also sorry for not being one.

Now, holding a bundle of mugworts in each one's arm which bore the weight of auspiciousness all the year round, June and May were walking on the way back home as well as in the Duanwu Festival. Their footsteps touching the memory and auspiciousness in my heart, I feel a tinge of pain.

《换水》

导 读

关于作者

李进祥，回族，宁夏同心县人，中国作家协会会员，宁夏作家协会副主席，被评为宁夏回族自治区"四个一批"文艺人才，宁夏回族自治区首批"塞上文化名家"。著有长篇小说《孤独成双》《拯救者》《绿叶红花》，小说集《换水》《女人的河》等，有数十篇作品入选《新华文摘》《小说选刊》《小说月报》及全国年度选本、中国短篇小说排行榜等。他的短篇小说《狗村长》获得由中国作家协会举办的"2007年全国读者最喜爱的小说奖"，入选《2007年中国小说排行榜》。短篇小说《四个穆萨》获"第六届鲁迅文学奖"提名。中短篇小说、散文分别获《小说选刊》奖、《飞天》十年文学奖、《回族文学》奖、黄河文学奖等。小说集《换水》获第十届全国少数民族文学创作"骏马奖"。《换水》收录了作者27篇短篇小说，讲述的是作者家乡清水河畔的故事。27个乡村人物故事充满了悲悯色彩，他们的人生际会、悲欢离合、生存状态都围绕着这条清水河的沉沉浮浮。他的作品以悲剧居多，其中《遍地毒蝎》《屠户》《口弦子奶奶》等篇目尤为精彩，文中所折射的思想和内涵令人深思。其中，《口弦子奶奶》被《小说选刊》选载。李进祥的小说文字朴素、风格家常，像一个未施粉黛的乡村姑娘，却散发着特殊的持久的清香，蕴意厚重。

关于作品

《换水》是真实生活的底片，描写了回族生活的细节。特别是那些描写女性柔美刚强的故事，在朴素寻常的面貌之下，有着让人不能小觑的穿透人性的艺术表现力。在这部作品中，有对乡土的痴恋与悲悯，有对人性的洞察与理解，有对命运的格外关注与不倦的追问。作品中的清水河是李进祥家乡真实存在的一条河流。"清水河"三个字听起来挺有诗意，实际上却是一条苦涩之河，既不能饮用，也不能浇地。时代的变迁和个体意识的觉醒，使那些不安于贫穷的清水河人产生了"冲出去"的渴望。然而，马清和杨洁却被城市鞭笞得遍体鳞伤，在城市中"丢失"了自我，最终选择了"逃离"。可以说，勤劳朴实的农民们逃离眼前的城市生活，并不是因为无能，而是因为不肯做金钱和利益的奴隶。李进祥关注中国社会转型时期农民所付出的心灵代价，他怀着一颗悲悯之心，注视着清水河畔的父老乡亲，叙述农民工五味杂陈的生活，探寻生命的意义。

译 文

Ablution

Li Jinxiang

Around the Qingshui River spreads a prevalent custom among Hui Muslims — one should have an Islamic ablution before going on a long journey.

"Huan Shui"(Chinese pinyin), a dialect, refers to having a full ablution, just like having a bath. However, it is tremendously different from bathing both in content and form. When it comes to having a bath, whether the head or the feet are washed first doesn't make any difference. Also, specifically speaking, taking a bath or a shower is all right. The only purpose is to keep clean. So, having a bath is casual, whereas "Huan Shui" is serious. As is tightly prescribed, one should have it with flowing water and in the right order. Besides, one should pay attention to how many times a certain body part is washed and which hand to use. Due to the strict procedures, it has become a holy or religious matter. Hence, "Huan Shui" can be revered as both a lifestyle and a religious form. Based on the rules, one should have an Islamic ablution every seven days, when attending Islamic services, having the Niyyah or going on a long journey.

"Get up for a full ablution, and let's start off early in the morning," said Ma Qing ("Ma" is the family name, while "Qing" the given name, the same Chinese character as "Qing" in "Qingshui River"). At that moment, he had the least laziness after the sexual activity, unlike before, but Yang Jie ("Yang" is the family name and "Jie" the given name) stayed motionless. Formerly, it was Jie who urged Qing to get up for an ablution before daybreak. He either drowsily stood still in the quilt or reluctantly had it with Jie. Now and then, it was something wrong with him. In that period, he would hug Jie for another time, funny and annoying, but she still lovingly maintained obedience.

Jie had been married to Qing just for three months. A new couple like them was always deeply attached to each other.

"What's going on? Once more?" Qing asked, with his hands cuddling around her.

"Ah, no!" Jie threw off his hands.

"Really go?" Jie responded with some doubts.

"You agree with me, right? Why say so?" Qing seemed impatient a little bit.

"I just..." She murmured in a low voice.

"You idiot! The town is equally a home to every man. People in the town have no red hair or green beard, haven't they?

We neither steal nor rob. Can't they swallow us? Hasn't everything been ok with me since I headed for a living in the town several years ago? Both building the house and marrying you depends on money I have earned there, right? I can't stand making a living at the mercy of Heaven for food." Qing presented so much at one go. He had repeatedly said this to Jie these days, so he blurted it out without any difficulty. Such facts seemed quite convincing.

  Jie got up with a coat wrapped around, poked the fire and heated up water. Though it was springtime, morning chills seemed so heavy.

  Qing was up very soon.

  The house was of slight silence, with water hissing in the kettle. For months, it had seldom remained so silent like this. Jie felt an inexplicable emptiness.

  "Can we have ablutions in the town?" While speaking it out, Jie herself saw it as ridiculous. Qing laughed as expected, "Do you think town people pay no attention to hygiene? Bathhouses of all sizes are available there. Actually, bath centers are set up to clean or soothe individuals' heads or feet. The sauna is a typical example. A variety of water heaters have found their way into every household. With a switch on, hot water is sure to come. It is fresh water, not as bitter as that of the Qing shui River. Now, you may figure out why their cheeks look so fair and clear? That depends on fresh water. If you go there, I can make sure that you look much better thanks to fresh water."

"You mean everything is ok with the town? Why not find a lover and live a town life but come back?" Jie pouted prettily, intending to mask the stupidity of her question. She had been asking such silly questions these days. Seeing peach trees in blossom, she asked, "Are there any peach trees? Do they bloom or not?" "Peaches are available all the year round, let alone peach trees." Qing said, "As long as you can afford them, you can have them anytime." "I mean 'peach blossom'!" Jie retorted. "Definitely yes! In the flower store there is anything you can expect. Even you can't name some flowers. On Valentine's Day, men will present roses, 20 yuan each, to women," Qing said. "You do so?" Jie choked him immediately. "How can I do that? If I earn money someday, I will buy roses specially for you," Qing said. "I don't care. I'm not your lover, whatever," Jie answered. No matter how silly questions were, they always ended up in Jie's success.

There were times when Qing was rendered speechless. "Is there the moon or stars in the town?" Jie asked. "Of course yes, but I haven't seen even once in the town," Qing responded, "the lamplight is so bright that radiance of the moon or stars is covered up." Jie was becoming complacent. Look, there are things invisible to the eyes of town people. From your perspective, the town can be compared to the paradise. That being said, she made up her mind to go with Qing. In fact, she also has a longing for the town. Though the farthest place she reached is the county, while on TV she witnessed urban life. She seems a little bit empty, so she asked again and again. What he said, like a hammer, tamped her belief little by little.

  Water boiling in the kettle was anxiously hopping. Since boiled water was ready, they two took turns for ablutions. As usual, Jie came first and took it more seriously than ever. Every step was put in place and appeared quite solemn, including rinsing the mouth, nose and hair. Having hung a water pot on the ceiling hook, Qing went out of the room and heard the long and solemn sound of flowing water. It was similar to what he heard when first leaving home for a living and passing by the Qingshui River. Layers of waves surged in his heart. Work experiences like a river were lively trickling from the bottom of his heart. He suddenly understood how Jie was feeling just then. He felt like a sense of empathy with her for the first time, which they lacked these days though passion was lingering. He put forth a renewed sense of love, compassion and tenderness. He said to himself, "I must protect her from being hurt. I must ensure her a decent life. "

  After the ablution, they packed the luggage, said goodbye to the family and started off. They first took the tricycle, then the shuttle bus and later the train. It took one day and one night to reach the destination. Qing seemed to know everything well and manage with ease. Qing tried to show off. Jie simply followed, getting on, taking a seat and getting off. At that time, she was more thrilled and bewildered than on the wedding day. Things were going much easier than he had expected. He found a job at the construction company he worked for last year. Before he returned home in winter, they reached an agreement that he could go on working when the company came into operation in spring. Also, they found a place to live in without too much effort. Because of urban expansion and renewal, there were plenty of bungalows to be dismantled nearby the construction site. People had moved somewhere else and the rent was not high. After one-day stay in the work shed, they moved to a newly-rented house, where water, a bed, several used cupboards and a coal furnace were available. Jie called it "home", and Qing followed suit. They bought a few simple pans and bowls in a nearby small shop, which unexpectedly brought about the "home" flavor. For Jie's part, everything went well like a sweet dream.

  The new house was not far away from the site where Qing worked and even that building could be seen in the yard. At work, he, as a bricklayer, could have a panoramic view of the small yard of their new house when doing some bricklaying and plastering on top of a scaffold. Thus, he gained a sense of belonging — belonging to the town — so that he could invest more strength and shoulder more responsibility. Even he felt as if he was working and building for his own sake. At the very beginning, he even hadn't missed his hometown. Formerly, he couldn't help looking towards the direction of his hometown during breaks at work. Knowing that nothing could be seen, he still sensed kind of sureness with a few glances. However, right now, in his eyes only remained the small yard in their new house. Off duty at noon, he promptly put away the trowel and the cutter, and then headed for home. Even though with much time after work in the afternoon, he was unwilling to stay for one more minute. Each time he got home, Jie had prepared face-washing water and dinner. Out of thrift, dishes were simple. Another reason was that they didn't know where to buy halal beef and mutton. Vegetables were something grown out of the land that whether Hui or Han people were able to eat, while meat couldn't be consumed at random. In spite of vegetarian dishes, they tasted delicious and satisfying.

Every day, Jie asked Qing to wash hair before sleep and helped him scrub his body. "I'm afraid that corrosive cement may lead to diseases." She said. Thus, Qing followed her will. He felt like a water heater, but Jie frowned upon that. "You can spend money like water, can't you?" she said, "This is not our own house, so it will be disassembled sooner or later. Take your time, and install it till we have our own house." Her words, like a current of air, blew up Qing's dream: a house of their own. He knew that it seemed rather distant, but he believed he had the determination, strength and wisdom to make the dream come true. However, so far, he had been in great need of a water heater because Jie was squeaky clean and loved washing. At home, she talked about heading for the Qingshui River to carry water as well as secretly have a bath without being seen by others. Qing also grew up in the surrounding areas of the Qingshui River, so when it came to Qingshui River, he could tell never-ending stories. They would be laughing while talking. Now, without TV for entertainment, they repeated those stories and jumped with joy all the same. Qing recalled the past event of pee matches when Jie turned angry and blamed, "People downstream fetch water there for drinking. Bad guy!" Jie lived in the lower reaches. Qing laughed, "Ha, you take a bath with my pee. No wonder you become my wife." Jie beat him with her fist. She said, "Water purifies itself as long as it runs. Running water is the best." She indeed felt homesick. She supposed it was largely because she had nothing to do but cook meals, wash clothes and wait her man back. She got used to doing something, so days like these were not her type.

"Is an unskilled laborer wanted on your building site?" Jie once asked.

"Definitely yes! What's up?" Qing had no idea.

"May I go to work there?" she replied in a direct manner.

"How can a woman do that?" Qing refused unhesitatingly.

Jie tried every possible way to persuade him, but he disagreed all along.

He dreamed of his wife living a life of a town woman rather than toiling away. He knew that so far he had no ability to bring her good days, but at least free her from sufferings. He tenderly loved and cherished her woman.

Their marriage was a traditional one, with the introduction of a matchmaker and the arrangement of the family. The good point was that they met several times before marriage and showed consent to each other. Deep down, he felt they were a perfect match as Qing knew about the name of Jie. Each youngster had something romantic in the mind. He agreed when they first met because she was so delicate and pretty that he firmly believed she was the right woman for him and saw it as love at first sight. After marriage, they were congenial to each other and lived in harmony so that Qing was wild with joy. He took Jie to the town. One wanted his woman to live a town life, while the other felt much attached to her man.

It was getting hot, the building Qing worked at taller, and the new house in his eyes smaller. Fortunately, he felt the real presence of Jie. He tried every means to please her. He spent 100 yuan buying an old TV set in an old electrical appliance store. Also, he made the antenna with cans on his own — although with few channels and vague pictures — she wasn't dull as ever. He picked up an inner tyre of a blender and made a solar water heater himself with which a shower was a daily possibility after a day's exposure to sunshine. Each of his inventions got her praise and kept her immersed in joy for a while. Qing felt content.

Qing said, "I swear some day I'll buy you a big house with a big color TV set and a real solar water heater."

Jie nodded with a smile, displaying her trust in her man. Qing also believed he could make it.

"Let's go home!" Jie said when she had just finished the latest ablution at their newly-rent house. Her hair was still wet, water drops streaming down her cheeks. She looked like being in tears. This newly-rent house would be pulled down tomorrow. After all, they had lived there for half a year. The sudden move left her sorrowful somehow. Jie accordingly said she had to take an ablution before moving. Actually, homesickness struck her again. Qing neither answered nor moved.

"Shall we go back? We have our own house and land there. We can live such a simple life just as others do. Back, ok?" Jie repeated.

"Shall we go back while I am in such a state?" Qing responded in an annoying and helpless tone.

Jie had no choice but to stop. His arm was injured.

He fell down from the scaffold and got this injury. He developed a habit of giving a few glimpses of their newly-rent house when building a wall for a while. There was a person he cared much about. She was the reason for his life and struggle, and the root he spared no effort to take in this town. The building was getting taller day by day, so were the surrounding ones. Hence, their new house seemed smaller and even out of sight. It was being swallowed by a group of buildings soon, so sometimes he had to stretch his neck hard, but only to see half of it. At one time, he exerted all his strength but in vain. He started to worry for fear that this small yard and Jie would be crowded out or even eaten up by the high-rise buildings. He industriously lifted his body as well as stretched his neck, but found nothing. Perhaps, as a result of strong wind, he suddenly fell down from the scaffold. If it had not been for the outside protective fence, he would have died. Thanks to it, he fell down from the distance of two-storey building, his arm clamped between the poles. Several workmates carried him down. They found he had just scraped the skin off his body, and scattered chatting and laughing. He had just slightly recovered from a recent fright, only to find that his right arm ached acutely with little strength. He asked for leave to the foreman and returned to the house. He appeared as if nothing special had happened, but Jie almost scared to death. She touched every part of his body and urged him to go to see a doctor. Qing said it was nothing wrong so that he could return to work the next day. However, in the same evening, his right arm swelled up and severe pains kept him sucking chill. Jie insisted on going to see a doctor, but he endured the pains and said that everything would be ok after a night's sleep. During this whole night, she kept warming the injured arm with a hot towel, but failed to reduce the swelling. She was getting worried, but had no clue about where the big hospital was. She once saw a small clinic with the curtain dotted with the shape of "the red cross" when buying vegetables, so she hurried to the clinic for a doctor's visit. Giving a few touches and pinches, the doctor said there was nothing serious with the bones but a little trauma. With the medicine taken, he would get better in a few days. He wore a professional look in a white doctor coat, so Jie felt like a relief. She went to the clinic and bought a lot of medicine. She followed the doctor's advice. After some washing, pasting and applying, she felt much at ease. Thanks to the pain killer, Qing was feeling a little better and took pains to go to the building site to report for duty. At first sight of his severely swollen arm, the foreman felt a little flustered. Any foreman would be afraid of accidents. On hearing that Qing was all right, he repeated, "Great! Have a good rest. You'll get paid as usual. The sooner you can recover, the sooner you will return."

  Some days later, the swelling of the arm was indeed reduced, so they two let out a big sigh of relief. Qing failed to raise this arm, but he believed he could get it over soon. He kept silent lest she should feel anxious. These days, Jie waited upon him and never came short in the smallest details such as feeding him something to eat or drink. He felt quite warm and believed it was advisable to take Jie out with him. Without her, it was hard to imagine how awful the situation would be. Just think of this, he reinforced the idea that he must be nice to Jie and bring good days to her. He thought he should make haste to go back to work till his arm was getting a little better.

  He recovered thoroughly and had no sense of pain, but his arm felt slightly stiff. This arm was not freely bendable — never reaching his face when he washed his face or his mouth when he had meals. He was bewildered, but tried to hide it from Jie. He held it might go along well after a full stretch over a few days' work. He went back to work. The foreman was happy to see Qing safe and sound, asking all over again, "Is everything ok?" Qing answered, "Sure." The foreman added, "The wage at shutdown can offset the medical fee. Everything is written off." They signed a new contract. After that, he climbed the scaffold again. Due to this fall, he became nervous, his hands and feet severely trembling. Taking his cutter and trowel out again, he restored the peace. He had worked as a brick layer for two or three years. He was so proficient in it that he had great confidence as soon as he took out the cutter. However, he managed with an effort to smear the mortar on the bricks, with his left hand pressing the bricks on the wall but his right hand not making the movements of knocking the bricks and scraping the ash. He failed each time and finally stopped. He didn't quit but continued with his left hand. Thus, the speed dropped by more than half. Others had built the wall quite high, but he ended up forming a gap. On the third day, his face taking on a ghastly expression, the foreman said in a "business-is-business" tone, "Go back and take a good rest. It was you who influenced the progress of the project. Come back when you recover. Welcome back anytime." The foreman led him down the scaffold and towards the office and counted out his wages more seriously. He reservedly said, "Have a rest, first. This time, no wage will be paid. If you don't go on, this contract will be canceled automatically." The foreman dangled that contract back and forth before his eyes. Without a single word, Qing came out and get confused. He walked back to their rented house with heavy strides, dropping hard upon the bed. Jie was frightened and came up to ask what had happened. He said he had been fired. Jie closely questioned why. Qing replied he couldn't work. With this out of his mouth, tears suddenly came out. Seldom did Jie see men shed tears. Think of the old saying that men's tears are as valuable as gold, and she got stuck in bewilderment in the face of this tear-streaming man. She rushed to put his head into her arms, and Qing trembled all over with sobs like a frightened child. At that time, she got the sense of the mother's arms around her own child. It was right then that she suddenly grew more mature and got a sense of responsibility. Regardless of the cost, she must heal his injured arm. The weakness of men tended to arouse the maternal instinct of women. Once it was activated, women would have iron nerves and never hold back when confronted with any difficulty.

Jie carried Qing, inquiring all the way about how to get to a big hospital. Finally, they made it to a true one, queuing up to register, seeing a doctor for a checkup and taking X-rays. She did everything as if she had been in town for ages. Conversely, Qing was like a new comer. He followed her timidly and mechanically.

The result of this checkup justified his timidity and worry. The doctor said, "This is the malposition of the bone mortise. The delayed adjustment should be responsible for the stubborn healing. An operation is a must now." "Will it heal properly?" Jie asked. The doctor said it should be ok after the surgery. "Is the fee high?" Qing asked. "No, it is about five or six thousand yuan."

Like a needle stabbing lightly, what the doctor said flung them into frustration. How to get five or six thous and? For months, he did earn several thousand yuan, but they only kept the living expenses, the rest sent to their native place. Arranging for the wedding and building the house had left them in debt.

This checkup made Qing clear, whatever. Every day he went out for a job. These years, he had worked outside, competent for any toilsome or arduous task such as carrying coal and shouldering jute bags. However, he clearly knew that he could no longer take on some of them. He had thought he was capable of doing it, only to find it was actually beyond him. In a short time, either the foreman or the owner would detest his clumsiness and fire him. He had no choice but to keep hunting for means of subsistence as well as being fired. Money he earned even couldn't support a family of two.

Jie also secretly went out for work, but she had no idea about what she could. The town was a pile of fog to her. She was born in a village and failed to complete the junior middle school, but she could deal with both farm and cooking work. As to town life, she just had glanced at it on TV. It was something that she really got envious of and yearned for. However, she didn't get well prepared mentally for how to survive the town. Sister Zhang, a plump woman from Gansu Province, had done some casual chatting about daily life with her, knowing that Jie did nothing, so she urged Jie to set a vegetable stall. Gansu was not far away from Jie's hometown and the accent was almost the same. She had a natural closeness to Sister Zhang whose stall she felt comfortable heading for. She knew Qing was against it. She herself was fearful, too. It ended up with nothing definite. This time, she made up her mind to have a try. She didn't turn to Sister Zhang for help because it was likely to cause some embarrassment or misunderstanding of her trying to "compete" with Sister Zhang. She felt his way to the dealer, aiming at wholesaling several types of vegetables, and displayed them for sale when she found she had neither the scales nor the plastic bags. She thought she might borrow the scales from the nearby stall if someone came up to her. Lowering her head all the time, she was left with nobody to care for it. Finally, there was a voice intended for her. It was not about buying vegetables but about asking for the stall. "What had happened? Why occupy my stall so rudely? Want to act with murderous intent? I haven't seen anyone fucking robbing me of it?" Shouted a tough and terrible-looking man. Jie, her face red, cleared away her vegetables and allowed room for her. She found another one again and felt like spreading them out when a woman vendor nearby came up to her, saying, "You are a green hand, right? This stall has been engaged. Place it where you rent, and don't take others' at will."

"Does it need to be rented?" Jie asked in a surprising tone.

That woman ridiculed, "Is anyone going to hand you a rent-free one? Nothing comes for free unless you are the lover of the administrator. The rent of land in the town is sky-high. A fucking small stall costs five thousand yuan per year. Damn it! Cruel!" Her rudeness evidently proved that she was not born there yesterday. Thus, Jie learned it was not easy to get going. She stood there at a loss. Just then, Sister Zhang came over and Jie became more upset. She, her head lowered and bundles of vegetables in her arms, intended to run away when Sister Zhang blocked her.

"Actually, I saw you earlier. I'm afraid that you will be embarrassed, so I dare not speak. The same is true for my first time. You will get used to it." Jie was blushing and speechless. After all, Sister Zhang was more experienced, and a sense of interdependence arose spontaneously.

  Sister Zhang drew near to her and asked about what had happened. She contributed an idea that Jie could buy a tricycle and make a mobile one, thus moving to the building sites or residential buildings. Besides, she was afraid that the vegetables would become a dead stock and helped transfer the vegetables Jie wholesaled at original prices. "There are still warm-hearted people in the world." Jie felt greatly grateful for what she had done. However, Jie couldn't afford a tricycle, nor could she ride it. She got into trouble. All of a sudden, she remembered her collecting water in the Qingshui River and got a brilliant idea. She didn't know where a shoulder pole could be bought, and casually used a stick. With strings tied at both ends, and each end tying a bamboo basket, a shoulder pole produced. The next day, Jie went to the small vegetable market again to wholesale some vegetables, carried them with a shoulder pole and wandered around the streets for sale. She failed to hawk her goods for the first time, and made it two days later. Once a woman left unchecked, she would be far tougher than a man. Her business was going well, so Qing had no sound reason to repeat his disagreement. However, she didn't want to do that on a long-term basis or make a big fortune. The only goal was to earn five or six thousand yuan and then cure Qing's arm.

However, by no means did she understand the rules of living. One day, when she carried the vegetable load, crying her vegetables for sale in an alley, several persons in uniform came over. In her eyes, people in uniform were policemen who caught bad guys. She just smiled. However, they looked gloomily serious and one of them harshly yelled at her, "who has allowed you to randomly cry for sale here?" Another one seized the scales in her hand before she could respond, and then relentlessly kicked over her two vegetable baskets, chilies and tomatoes rolling down the ground. Yang crazily rushed up, tightly caught hold of one hand of a person in uniform, and then severely gripped it with her teeth, making him soaring with pain. The other two took much trouble to pull her away. Later on, she learned that those in uniform came from the section of urban administration and specially supervised the phenomena of disorderly setting marketing stalls to avoid spoiling the cityscape. She had never imagined she would get so irritated that she dared to bite his hand. The result was that she was pushed and shoved to the section of urban administration, fined and almost sent to the local police station.

She couldn't manage to run this stall, and never knew what to do next. Just then, the rented house was to be pulled down so that she actually desired to go home.

However, Qing refused to do so. It wasn't because he had not such an idea but he couldn't. In doing so, whether before the villagers or the women, he could no longer raise his head. He, to some extent, was not resigned to this. Another reason was that he got a family letter saying his younger brother had been admitted to a university with high tuition of more than ten thousand yuan, and he was required to try every possible way to gather five thousand yuan. He kept it secret that his arm was severely injured, but explained he was not paid. He asked his family to borrow money first, and sent it back upon drawing the salary. His brother's schooling was a big event. He hoped that his brother could be free from walking around for extra opportunities.

He had to bear the sufferings

"After an ablution, let's go home!"

Half a year later, Qing offered to go home. During this period, they rented another house; Qing ended up with a fixed one after trying a dozen of jobs; Jie first worked as a dishwasher and waitress in a Lanzhou Halal Noodle Restaurant, and then washed hair in a barbershop, and finally seemed to find a permanent job. Jie said nothing about what she was doing, neither did Qing ask her. Qing made no reply at all.

Qing worked as a cleaner in a restaurant, sweeping the floor, mopping the floor and flushing the toilet. It was not hard to get it.

When applying for it, he frankly revealed his disability because he knew that truth would come out anyway. Unexpectedly, the boss said happily, "Disabled! Oh, don't be afraid! When I came out of the country, I first worked in a factory where an ingot broke my leg. For all that, I hewed out my career." "Guy, don't lose heart and do your best. No cross, no crown." He also urged, rolling up his trousers, half an artificial limb exposed. Qing was accepted. He knew that quite a few people who came from the country made money in the town. He never dreamed of making such a big fortune as the boss did. Even the thought of settling down in the town hadn't entered his mind at all. If only the debt of building his house for marriage and supporting his brother for tuition could be paid off! He, a 1.8-meter-tall man, lay on his stomach, mopping the floor. He first felt wronged, but gradually got used to it. After all, earning money was of more importance than earning face. Despite a water-flush toilet with white ceramic tiles inlaid, it throws off a strong smell. It went worse, especially when the pipe was blocked. Again, he got used to it. Alas, Poor thing! He didn't tell it to Jie, and actually took no opportunity. During this time, Jie changed another job, out before dark and not back till the next morning. He chanced to be out in the morning and back after ten o'clok each night. Thus, they two seldom met.

In spite of this, each time Qing was off duty, he would first take a bath at a bathhouse, which was nearby his rented place, kind of shabby and charged low —— only three yuan. Even so, he ached for that. He didn't want to bring home a bad smell, for he couldn't bear Jie smelling a bit of stink. Strictly following the procedures of the ablution, he completely washed out each part of the body. The length of bath time was also ensured. Town water was sweet, but too soft to keep things thoroughly clean. Conversely, water in the Qingshui River was salty, but strong enough to keep everything thoroughly clean. There seemed to be a stream of momentum! With a suit of clean clothes put beforehand in the bathhouse, he put them on after the ablution and then went home. The next morning, he made his way to the bathhouse for his work clothes. The bathhouse boss permitted it. Not seeing Jie, he insisted on doing this and never treated it lightly.

  Seemingly, Jie also took a bath before going home, which Qing never saw but sensed through Jie's pillow with the flavor of the shampoo and some water marks. Qing held it in his arms while asleep every night. He couldn't figure out whether the marks are water in her hair or tears in her eyes. Jie, a delicate woman, seldom shed tears, even when those who accompanied her to Qing's family returned on the wedding day. Jie once came back at midnight, tears streaming down her cheeks. She bathed again and again with cold water. Qing asked her about what had happened, but she washed tearfully without a single word. Qing could do nothing but leave her alone. He tried to hug her and asked again, but such a touch, like a stab, had her scream. She rolled up the quilt and turned around, ceaselessly trembling all over. Qing had no idea, and believed she had known his job and then looked down upon him. He slept, kind of angry and helpless.

Clothes and cosmetics in the room could tell that Jie had loved making up. He could never associate such fashionable clothes with Jie, for she had long been simple and plain. He had hoped to take Jie to the town and dress her up, but later couldn't imagine what she would be like in such clothes. With a good look and a nice figure, Jie must be pretty and lovely in those, but in Qing's eyes, if so, Jie would be another unknown woman. Also, he found an eyebrow pencil and a lipstick. It was even harder to imagine the way she was with her eyebrows penciled and her lips colored. All of a sudden, he thought of that kind of woman in the town who put on too much makeup. They were called "Ji"(namely Chinese Character "鸡": a type of domesticated fowl, also referring to "prostitute"). Most of them were from the country, where men make a living by selling their sweat, while women by their bodies. What a humble life! Some peasant-workers paid for that, but Qing was unwilling to do the same with hard-earned money. He showed mercy, but more disgust. He dared not associate Jie with those women. He believed her.

After another period of time, Qing came back home one evening and surprisingly found Jie also in. She seemed to specially wait for him and cook dinner for him. Dinner done, Jie suddenly took out a pile of money, excitedly saying, "Let's go to see a doctor tomorrow and return home when you recover." Qing asked how she had made so much money, only to find that her face clouded. "I didn't steal or rob it. I made it on my own!" she defended. "Oh, OK! Just send it off to pay the debt. Nothing wrong with my arm," he replied. Her eyes were lacking in luster.

Qing sent money back home the next day. Money out, worry in. He wondered why she suddenly made so much and what on earth she was doing. He knew he shouldn't be suspicious, but couldn't help wondering... "Find time to talk with her," he said to himself.

The house was in a mess. Jie was dazzledly lying on the bed, her face flushed and straggly hair wet. She seemed ill. Qing went forward to touch her forehead, only to find that she was running a high fever. "What's wrong?" he asked. "Perhaps... a bad cold," Jie answered with difficulty. Since they two seldom met during this period, they became more unfamiliar and more polite so that they would be not like a couple. Qing said, "Let me take you to hospital." "Never mind. Just take some medicine," Jie gasped out, "go to the clinic in the lane and buy some medicine, please." When it came to a small clinic, Qing flew into a rage. "A small clinic? Damn it! Let's go to a hospital." Jie refused. He had no choice but to go out for medicine. There was no certified pharmacy and it was getting dark, so he bought several kinds of medicine in that small clinic. Jie took it, but didn't feel better. After midnight, her condition worsened. She had quite a high temperature, sometimes screaming, sometimes shouting and then laughing. Qing never heard such laughter with a puff of frivolity, which he felt disgusted about. However, affection and pity welled up in his heart as he saw her sickly look.

At daybreak, Jie wasn't getting better. Qing was so worried that he sent her to a nearby hospital, where he was on the run first from the department of Internal Medicine, then to Gynecology and finally Venereology. He didn't think too much, but went through the formalities and arranged for a bed.

Jie had been in hospital for five days, sometimes conscious and sometimes unconscious for the first three. When fully conscious on the fourth, she insisted on leaving hospital, while Qing staying for another day. Also, the doctor urged, "It takes time. Be patient." Jie responded, "Money is a big headache." Thus, they left.

Back to the rented house again, they never felt at home in such a cold and messy place. Having helped her up to the bed and wrapped her up with a quilt, he hastened to make a fire. Early spring in the city was still exceptionally cold. With fire, chill was squeezed out of the house bit by bit. Then, he put a kettle of cold water, and soon heard the kettle sizzling. They hadn't been with each other like this for long. Either of them uttered no word. Jie started first in a faint voice, "We have been here for one year. It's like a dream." Qing kept silent. After a while, Jie continued, "I tried saving up some money to cure your arm, but it is me who have spent it." Qing was still silent.

The kettle was sizzling.

"Let's take an ablution and go home," Qing said suddenly.

Surprisingly gazing at him, Jie said with uncertainty, "Really?"

"Definitely yes! Go home! Tomorrow!" he responded in a cool but firm tone.

"Can we be back? Look at me..." she asked nervously.

"Stop it! Go home first!" Qing seemed to be afraid of changing his idea owing to what Jie would say.

They were speechless, again.

Water was ready, so the house was getting warm. They took turns to have an ablution —— first Jie and then Qing. Recalling their one-year-ago ablution and entering the city, they had an indescribable taste. Just out of hospital, Jie was rather weak, so Qing poured water down her body. He found wounds and scars throughout her body, and even traces of burnt cigarettes. Suddenly, tears came out. He was choking, "It's all my fault. I shouldn't have taken you out. Almighty water in the Qingshui River can wash any disease away. Go home!" Droplets flowed all over her face and body. Water or tears? Who can tell?

《赛麦娘的春天》

导　读

关于作者

马金莲，女，回族，80后，宁夏西吉县人。中国作家协会会员，鲁迅文学院第22届高级研讨班学员。2000年开始文学创作，作品以中短篇小说为主。先后在《作品》《天涯》《十月》《花城》《北京文学》《清明》等刊物发表作品近300余万字，部分作品被《小说选刊》《小说月报》《新华文摘》《作品与争鸣》《北京文学·中篇小说月报》《中华文学选刊》《散文选刊》《散文海外版》等转载，多篇作品入选全国性年度文学选本。其代表作品有小说《掌灯猴》《春风》《父亲的雪》《老人与窑》《糜子》《永远的农事》《鲜花与蛇》《夜空》等。著有小说集《父亲的雪》《碎媳妇》《长河》《1987年的浆水和酸菜》《绣鸳鸯》《难肠》等，以及长篇小说《马兰花开》《数星星的孩子》。中篇小说《长河》获"2013年度中篇小说评选"第一名，被誉为当代的《呼兰河传》。长篇小说《马兰花开》获第十三届精神文明建设"五个一工程"奖。另外，还曾获《民族文学》年度奖、《小说选刊》年度奖、首届朔方文学奖、郁达夫小说奖、首届茅盾文学新人奖、第十一届全国少数民族文学创作"骏马奖"等。马金莲在观察、描绘和体悟宁夏回族生活的文化特质、精神内涵及价值取向等方面，笔触细腻，构思巧妙，其作品表现出独特的思想意蕴和强大的艺术感染力。

关于作品

"赛麦"是回族人特有的名字。《赛麦娘的春天》以女性的视角，朴实细腻的笔调，生动凝练的汉语，以及地道精妙的宁夏西海固方言，描绘了宁夏回族普通民众特有的生存状态和精神状态。文中多次出现"碎"这个字，如："……外奶奶睡着在墙根下，她的头靠着土坯，白头发从手巾缝里溜出几根，在微风里晃，一双碎脚放在花荫深处。""碎"是典型的宁夏西海固方言，读来让人感觉亲切天然，纯净美好。作者具有强烈的民间意识和出色的艺术审美能力，感情真挚、观察细致、描摹精致，展现了一幅具有浓郁地方色彩的风情图景，表现了回族人积极乐观的精神气质。

译 文

The Spring of Syme's Mother

Ma Jinlian

　　Spring is always pacing so hesitantly that people are too impatient to wait.

　　The dry and chilly wind throughout the winter blew till the end of the first lunar month, giving some illusion that spring will never arrive. However, some day in February, you will unexpectedly find in the corner or at the roadside a cluster of sharply-pointed wheatgrass shoots or several leaves of wild plants sheepishly popping their heads out, which offers you a pleasant surprise, and convinces you of the real and eventual arrival of spring. Spring is like a consistently unkempt woman, who is believed to be never neat, but one day suddenly shows up in front of you, clean, mild-looking and seemingly complacent after playing tricks.

　　This weather once dusted the eyes of Syme.

　　In Syme's eyes, the wind lasted the whole winter. The northwest wind howled day and night. Therefore, Syme could do nothing but play with her younger brothers and sisters on the kang (a heatable brick bed in North China) all day. There were only three snowfalls all winter, accounting for Syme's impression of ceaseless wind this winter. The wind blowing across bare branches made peals of rustles and the lifted tiles kept up an endless crack when the wind blew over the roof. Listening to the dreadful wind, Syme couldn't help yearning for spring. If only spring could approach earlier! At least, the vernal wind wouldn't blow off the tiles. Alas! Where is spring going? If impatient, Syme was starting to nurse a hatred for spring.

  Just in early February, Syme saw her mother warming eggs. Mother raised eight hens and two cocks. In addition to laying a few eggs each day, they did nothing but dug up a pile of ash manure in the backyard, making their feathers jumbled like a group of beggars. While warming eggs, Mother wore a mysterious smile on the face. She placed a cylindrical tube made of old barks at the corner of a kang, with chicken feathers stuffed in half a tube. The hens having finished laying eggs, the eggs, while hot, were collected and put among the chicken feathers as soon as possible so that they could cuddle up with each other to keep warm. The picture of smooth eggs lying together naturally called to Syme's mind whether she was set among her siblings for warmth by Mother as a kid. In that case, she was kind of an egg, wasn't she? Such a wild idea made Syme feel both annoyed and funny. When Syme witnessed what her mother had done, Mother winked back at her and then murmured that Syme should keep her lips zipped. Afterwards, Mother left with a cordial and trustful smile. However, this weighed heavily on her mind due to her unintentional encounter of Mother's secret, which Mother clearly pled with her to keep. Syme was getting indescribably so excited that she felt like pushing the chicken feathers aside to review those eggs, but holding it back in the end.

The bark tube used to warm eggs remained a knot in Syme's heart. She glanced over it from time to time, and couldn't help reaching out to touch and count them. Although kept among the chicken feathers, the eggs cooled. It was natural that Syme naturally began to worry about whether cold eggs could hatch chickens or not. She put it forward while Mother added eggs inside. At that time, seriously tilting her head and lifting her chest, It was natural that Syme watched her mother and said, "Mother, can such cold eggs hatch chickens? What if a nest of water eggs are hatched, what shall we do?" Syme felt quite complacent because she thought she had been aware of it. Such complacency uncontrollably crept up to her face. She was really fearful that if a nest of water eggs were hatched, how Mother could confess to Father? Thinking of this, Syme held she was virtually saving her mother. However, Mother looked at Syme and roared with laughter. It seemed that what Syme said was very ridiculous. Silly girl! Mother patted on Syme's head and then laughingly went out. Syme touched her own face, kind of feverish, and seemingly worried too much.

Syme found that the eggs the big hen laid were light red, while those the small silkie laid were white. Besides, the eggs the small hen laid were much bigger than those the big hen did. How werid! The big hen is unexpectedly inferior to the small one. Most probably, the big barred rock hen merely looked like an empty frame. Hence, Syme was a little resentful to that big barred rock hen while feeding them.

In fact, it was obviously too early that the chickens could be hatched in early February. It was very hard for them to survive the intense cold. Syme visited several neighbors, not only for amusement but also on purpose. During the visits, she never forgot to glance at the corner of the kang in others' houses, only to find that there were no bark tubes except a stack of well-folded quilts or an unfolded mattress.

Syme silently counted all the boxes, baskets, basins and jars which could be used to warm eggs. Finally, she safely drew the conclusion that women in the village had not yet warmed eggs — even without a little sign. Full of pride, Syme thought, "Wait to see! Lazybones! When you get ready for it, Mother's chickens can run around."

It was just a few days before two dozens of eggs had been warmed. Much to Mother's excitement, a hen had stayed still in its house for a few days, indicating that it was building a nest for the hatched chickens. It was time! Syme knew the eggs Mother collected could make a nest of chickens. This was a lean pheasant, who once laid several eggs, but not eye-catching, so Syme didn't notice it much. The pheasant who had built the nest was no longer timid, with the feathers all over the body standing on end like a duster. It bent over the rick and stayed firm. When Syme tried to drive it away, it flapped the wings, sending out "cluck-cluck", as harsh as the sound of shabby brushes brushing wood. It steadfastly guarded the nest, motionless. It was this humble lean hen that first built a nest. The whole family felt rather amazed and treated it as meritorious. The pheasant having crouched into the house that Mother made, it became ill-mannered to human at all once, guarding against human with fierce looks, just like a shrew. A score of eggs were in full put under the body of the hen. Nevertheless, Syme perceived its insuppressible delight and excitement from its cautious sight. It was raising its own chickens.

  The pheasant did have profound thoughts and endurance to loneliness, which Syme soon found out. Though trying not to keep thinking about it, she was unable to restrain herself from paying more attention to it while feeding hens. She noticed that the pheasant, lying over twenty eggs, remained motionless for long, the little eyes glowing with long and dreamy light. It looked like a dozing old man in the warm sun, calm and tired. All eggs, like sleeping babies, lay under the body of the hen, who unfolded its two wings to the greatest extent to cover them tightly. On seeing the hens' sparing no effort to protect the chickens, Syme felt cheerful and supposed whether Mother brought up her children just like that. More often, the pheasant closed its eyes. Syme cautiously slipped into the house and peeked, only to find that the pheasant was sleeping. Oh, was it actually sleeping? And wasn't it afraid that the eggs would be stolen? The sleeping pheasant looked quite distressed, the slightly –astringed eyelid seemingly heavy, the bony head kind of motionless upright snakehead, the comb overhead seeping with light blood. Its color was far from red and gaily when it laid eggs. Syme worried, "if left unchecked, can the pheasant hold on to the last and make it? For twenty–one days, as shut in a cell, can the poor little hen survive?"

The house was very quiet. The sky, the wind blowing over, was cloudless. The sun, as if veiled by dust, gave out dim light and fell aslant the windowsill. Syme sensed that the hubbub of the younger brothers next door seemed unreal, especially in such weather, and everything was empty and depressing. Suddenly, mingled with melancholy, Syme softly grabbed a handful of wheat into the bowl near the pheasant. Awake, it vigilantly watched Syme and blinked its little eyes. Mother calculating day by day, close to the 21st day, the chickens were about to come out. In this respect, Syme thoroughly admired Mother. When asked about it, Mother could blurt out without second thoughts. She knew the dates as well as her ten fingers and palm prints. Syme viewed it as Mother's another talent. On the morning of 25th, February, She learned that one chicken came out the day before and till morning, the other seven did. Later, all the eggs cracked with small triangle holes were knocked, damp and pasted with sticky blood and yellow water when just fished out of water. Mother quickly put them into heaps of cotton for warmth. Mother said it was already 25 days since the fourth day of the second lunar month. Therefore, she put the last two eggs without any sign of birth into the paddy basket and observed them, her neck stretching long and eyes staring firmly. "Have you noticed whether these eggs moved?" Mother asked. Syme, very funny, stretched her neck, like a thin hemp rope. Mother looked quite nervous, her face drawing closer and closer to the paddy basket. Syme found Mother naughty and lovely at that time. After a while, Mother stood up, rubbed her eyes, and said, "My dazzling eyes don't work. Can you check it for me?" Accordingly, Syme hunted for those two eggs. Syme said to herself, "You two! Mother didn't see them clearly because she might shed tears into the wind. Let me make it." She felt as if they were playing hide-and-seek. However, Mother let out a sigh at Syme's ear, fairly warm, "It looks like water eggs. Take it and play with it." Mother herself, and even Father never noticed her worn-out clothes. The tender feathers all over the chickens' body seemed completely fluffy. Running back and forth, they were mistaken for fur bulbs rolling at first sight. The chickens kept clucking, like chattering together. Syme considered them quite cute, and tender as if elutriated in the water. Thus, the family were somewhat getting all the more soft and bright. At that time, Mother told what she wanted in a calm manner obviously because she had thought it over and over. She let out a sigh, not long but melancholy and unutterable. At a time, distracted from the chickens, everyone was watching Mother and wondered what was on her mind.

Pulling the front of her clothes, Mother said, "Alas, I'm afraid that it is six years since I had the clothes. How time flies! They appear worn-out and I even have no decent clothes." Awaken by that, they began to look Mother's clothes up and down. Syme considered Mother totally right and her clothes too old-fashioned to last. The previous jacket dotted with vivid clover blossom faded into grey now. If dressed in such ones, Mother would be much paler and shorter. Actually, she was tall and not so old.

Syme found Mother did it on purpose. She meant it this time because she didn't make any request for her own sake. Since she spoke it out, she must have had her own idea.

"I want to sell the nest of chickens. Wait till they grow a

bit." Mother added.

"That sounds great! The chickens can sell at a high price if earlier. I chance to buy the chemical fertilizer with the money. It's my big headache these two days." Father said approvingly. "Oh, no! Don't count on it. I want to buy new clothes." Mother said anxiously. She hurriedly expressed her request on the ground that all considered her clothes too shabby. In the following long period, Syme often observed Mother's busy legs and imagined what trousers Mother would buy. Since Syme had memory, the cloth called "Panama" had been popular in the village. An aunt once had a pair of blue trousers made of "Panama". Syme remembered that as long as she went out, she would put on her "Panama", her legs keeping upright, asking Mother out together outside the gate. Now, "Panama" has been out of date. In the ageing of Mother and the aunt, and the growth of the children, the unforgettable "Panama Times" for the aunt eventually passed away. However, Syme was not sure about what clothes Mother preferred.

I

Mother set about cleaning the house and yard, and unpicking and washing the bedding, which indicated that our new life was coming. I couldn't clearly explain what our new life was like and how to live it, but I knew for sure we would really live a new life. The changes, in and out, proved that. So did Mother's delight on her dusty face. On a warm and sunny noon, the preparatory work finally fell on us. Mother boiled a large basin of water for us so that we could have a thorough bath, wash away the body dirt saved up all winter, and then put on the clothes Mother had unpicked, washed, sewed and mended.

Mother removed a large pile of broken bricks and tiles at the gate to the backyard, and put them as tidily as the orderly bowls and chopsticks. The door of the big house was decorated with a new white door curtain embroidered with red flowers. Seeing these small but concrete changes, breathing the musty smell of the old cloth after being unpicked and washed and the smell of dust bouncing and falling in the cleaning, we felt a bright future close to us. A new life was somewhat clear, and seemingly around the corner.

The 12th day of the second lunar month was a good day, the sky very azure like a handsome face covering overhead, the sun quite gentle coming out as trippingly as the relative-visiting pace. On getting up in the morning, parents again swept the house inside and outside. Very often, only when sweeping the floor for several times could they feel content. In fact, the house was tidy, but the yard could never be kept clean because gusts of wind always blew away dust, chicken feathers, rotten grass, etc., swirling in the center of the yard. Therefore, we had no choice but to sweep it for a few more times. Even if clean for a while, it was better.

It was Father who cleaned the yard. He had rarely been so diligent before and thoroughly swept every corner never done at ordinary times. The new door curtain swayed on and on with the wind, a delicate fragrance of incense sticks wafting out of the door and filling the air in the yard. Having cleansed the hands and faces, we were playing the game of "Tiao Fang" in the yard. We also felt freshness of a new life because Mother watched us with sufficient praise.

It was just on this day that our grandma arrived.

Upon her arrival, our new life set out.

Grandma came on a donkey — a small black donkey, dressed like a new groom, wrapping up a small cyan quilt with a saddle of red wood, under which two small stirrups hung, golden and sparkling in the sunshine. Putting her small feet on the golden stirrups all the way, Grandma staggered her way across the mountain and ditch from my aunt 20 li away to my home.

II

Grandma's feet were really so small that she limped along into our house with Mother's support after getting off the donkey. Supposedly, her feet were only a span of my small hand long, like two steamed buns, not round or flat, covered with layers of white cloth, and wrapped around by a pair of small and exquisite cloth shoes of black velvet. Hence, what terrified people was that her shoes were also unusual — only a span long, narrow and pointed. How could such a tall granny wear so small shoes? How could she stand such pain?

Grandma seemed nothing wrong. On getting off the donkey, she gaily smiled, and loudly greeted those who came out to meet her. She was really old, her weather-beaten face disorderly lined with dense wrinkles, which divided her face into countless lumps— so frightening that one dare not see it. Very soon, I found her wrinkles not messy but clear and sharp. Her face was brown yel low, her cheeks sunken, her mouth tightly compressed, and her nose looking big and round, like a small well-cooked steaming potato.

Grandma wanted to touch our faces. Mother pushed us one by one to her. I was after my sister, whose hands felt dry and hard, like a thorn pricking my face. The sound of cutting skins and fleshes of broken tiles rang in my heart. She was serious and gracious, the corner of her mouth wiggling as if saying something. While her rough hands touched the face of my younger brother, I figured out all faces were safe and sound, not oozing any blood as we feared. I saw our faces glowingly red, and sensed our hearts filled with happiness and shyness. In our hearts flashed a trace of sadness that we had been forsaken so long before dearly loved with Grandma's touch.

Our grandmother's big hands felt so rough, making us shedding tears inside.

The grandmother brought us a large package of tasty food. Our new life really started.

III

On hearing Grandma's arrival, Great grandfather rushed to our home.

"Bang-bang" was getting around in the distance before he arrived.

Knocking the walking stick all the way, Great grandfather moved slowly.

Compared with Great grandfather, we found Grandma much younger. Mother said he was eighty years old, while Grandma said he was over ninety. "One can stick around for a few more days each year, but your great grandfather has been hanging on for many years. I'm afraid he didn't know for sure. Alas, there is no sign of 'Wu Chang' (A religious term, meaning 'death') How annoying! " Grandma said, lips curled and re vealing a wearisome look.

In fact, even if so young, we could read Grandma's anxiety

that Great grandfather had so long a lifespan and never showed the sign of departure. It seemed true. If one was still alive in the 80s or 90s, he or she would be a dotard. They might as well make their own leave. Otherwise, how embarrassing it was to stick around in the future generations and be waited on by our grandma!

However, there was completely no sign of dying. Instead, he was all the more healthy and robust. On hearing Grandma's arrival, he rushed over despite much inconvenience.

They held hands like kids, four old hands clasping tremblingly for long.

"You are alive, aren't you?" Grandma asked, in a high voice.

"Alive! Alive! Kids must be impatient." Great grandfather almost screamed, also in a high voice.

A houseful of people burst into laughter, amused by Great grandfather. He laughed, too. The two seniors' faces revealed childlike naughty looks. They smiled face to face, shedding very turbid tears.

Great grandfather came from Grandma's mother's home. At this encounter, he said with a sigh, "I can't imagine seeing you at such an advanced age."

Due to Grandma's arrival, he didn't chat with others. The two seniors climbed up the kang, leaned against the wall and talked along. In fact, their chat was too dull to attract the listeners. Great-grandfather's white beard was trembling, and his clear drivel falling down to the tip of beard and hanging in the air. Grandma's sunken mouth was moving slowly, and also the clear drivel hanging on the tip of her nose. She stood still while talking. It was long before she suddenly perceived it and then hurriedly drew the towel out of the pocket in the chest part of her clothes to wipe it off.

What the two seniors who couldn't hold back drivels said never aroused our interest. Sometimes, Grandma was listening as Great-grandfather talked, while sometimes, Great-grandfather was listening as Grandma talked. The talker uttered slowly, while the listener nodded vigorously. At times, they laughed together, as in high spirits as kids.

Grandma said, "Did you remember that I waited for you till the sunset at the gate of the old yard when you begged out for food with a wool bag? Later, you returned with a package of stuff when I jumped with joy. But I opened it, only to find a stone. We seemed to sleep hungry that night." Speaking of this, Great grandfather spontaneously touched his belly, as if it were still empty until now.

Great-grandfather said, "I chop the tail of Wang Fuhan's dog, and you got several lashes for it."

Grandma said, "When my kids were almost starved to

death, it was you who brought a package of naked oats and saved their lives. Later, I knew you had gotten the deduction of rations and even failed to eat the flour-made food."

All of these were very, very old, but surprising us now and then. They talked and laughed like kids, as if they had gone back several decades ago to the youthful time.

Every three or five days, Great grandfather would come over so as to chat with Grandma.

Having sent Great grandfather away, Grandma went to the corner of the yard to level the ground. Our yard was spacious and empty. Mother talked of growing vegetables each year, but never took actions. On her arrival, Grandma insisted, "Anything you plant will do. If the ground is left deserted, it is a pity." Grandma decided to plant flowers in our yard. She had the flower seeds herself. She wore a traditional Chinese bellyband next to the skin with two incredibly big pockets, which were so full that her belly bulged. She lifted up her clothes and pulled out a paper parcel. When it was unpacked, a wide range of flower seeds came out. Now, I knew that Grandma always had some flower seeds with her and planted some wherever she went.

Nobody cared about how to dig and level the ground, and plant the flowers. Parents worked in the mountain and the kids played here and there. No one took notice what Grandma had done when looking after the house for us. For the whole spring and over a half of the summer, parents had been busy working in the field, my elder sister tending sheep and other kids playing outside. We left the house to Grandma. We were not confined to the house as usual but far freer, because she took care of the house, dogs and chickens. The whole spring and over a half of the summer elapsed very fast. Only when seeing the blooming of flowers did we surprisingly realize that Grandma had not only looked after the house for us but also planted flowers.

IV

Flowers seemed to be blooming overnight. We weren't home until it was getting completely dark. We slept through the night. Stepping out of the house, we amazingly found flowers coming out. It was overnight that many flowers bloomed.

 These flowers were beautiful and rare. One white kind, as big as the palm, smells pale, even without a little delicate fragrance. Its petals were so thin that brightness could pass them through. Grandma said it was named "Seven-leaf flower". Another purple kind of seven-leaf flowers looked so eye-catching that they could be seen blooming in the distance. One golden kind named "Erigeron breviscapus" flourished and looked the most attractive, a row trimly blooming in the distance, and the sweet flavor unceasingly wafting out. What alluring aromas!

Flowers seemed so many that the yard was getting full and boisterous. The empty yard appeared crowded and even a little narrow. I enjoyed the flowers, my younger brother kept in the dark. We walked back and forth in the flower shrubs. Grandma cautiously came over and repeatedly warned us, "Don't break off the flowers! Don't tread the stems!" Dressed in cyan Chinese traditional clothes, her head wrapped with a white towel, her nose turning red, Grandma happily walked up and down in the yard. The flowers Grandma planted were in boom. She had been here only for half a year and she had the deserted yard fully decorated with flowers. I had never seen some flowers before. We virtually had to regard this old and skinny granny with special respect.

The bees flew up one after another with sweet flower fragrance. At high noon, if you sat under the flowers and listened carefully, you could hear hums and buzzes, and see them noisily haunting among the flowers. They must be overwhelmed with joy. Like us, they were brought up in the village and had never seen the flowers before. It was true that we hadn't seen many flowers before, neither had the adults.

On hearing that, the kids rushed over. Like us, they had dirty hands, dirty faces, and dirty worn-out clothes covered with mud and grass juice. Mouths wide open, they stared at our flowers, one of whom reached out to the flower while no one noticed, which was a white seven-leaf flower, calmly gazing at people. He almost reached the flower when I stopped him. His dirty hands betrayed he had played with mud in the ditch. How could we allow such dirty hands to touch our flowers?

The kid consciously shrank back his hands, but bumped against the stem with one trembling hand. The flower wobbled violently when another kid immediately screamed and gloated, "Sheba is breaking off the flower."

Grandma rushed over with her halting small feet.

"Wow——", Sheba howled.

Grandma stayed speechless on account of astonishment. Sheba cried towards the seven-leaf flower, his dirty hands plastered with tears streaming down his dirty face, his mouth wide open. Obviously, he was too frightened to do anything but cry.

However, Grandma didn't blame for it.

"Oh, don't cry, please! Nobody says you broke off the flower. Do you see it? Sheba just wants to pull the flower in a gentle manner. Go ahead! No one will scold you." Grandma said loudly with a smile.

Sheba licked his dry and scaly lips, glanced at Grandma, held back his cry, nodded and whispered, "I just want to pull them, not to break them off." Sheba's hands, like bony chicken claws, and just having dug up the dung and dirt, were tremblingly reaching out to our flowers. Grandma approvingly watched his behavior with her smile lingering on, but we were extremely anxious and uneasy because Grandma allowed Sheba to play with flowers with his dirty hands. How annoying! But Grandma was ready for it.

The flower was trembling a little, so was my heart. The pure white petal in his hand, Sheba seemed very nervous, and even out of breath. Later, Sheba reached out two fingers, straightly touched the petal and quickly released it. The flower was moving slightly, no dirty mud pasted with it, so I breathed a sigh of relief. Suddenly, Sheba crazily headed towards the gate, where he cried and ran away.

Kids burst into laughter at Sheba's weird behavior. So did I. But Grandma didn't. Her lips compressed, her face wearing tiredness, Grandma moved into the house with small paces.

After a while, other kids watched the flowers and then slipped away. When everyone was gone, we were shocked to see that some flowers had been missing. The broken ones were almost very big and flourishing. Several tall stems lowered their heads and some leaves messed away. The broken flowers gazed at Grandma with great frustration.

It really happened beyond Grandma's expectation. She had a look at the flowers, the kids, and then turned to the flowers. The younger sister felt wronged and said, "I haven't got one, but outsiders broke them off. How hurt!" This was indeed what I wanted to say. The younger brother longed for one, but Grandma firmly refused, just allowed him to touch the petals and then drove him away. Grandma said, "Whoever dares to break off the flowers must be severely punished." Her utterances frightened and stopped us, but other kids broke so many flowers. How could we stand it? So hurt! Most of all, we were angry with Grandma because it was she who allowed Sheba to pull the flowers and then boost other kids' courage.

Grandma watched the flowers for some time and said, "Alas, my kids! How can you do that?" Inhaling as if with a toothache, Grandma found some sticks to prop up the damaged stems.

Grandma decided to present some flower seeds to every household in the village. Flowers continuously blooming and fading, various seeds grew in shape and ripe very soon. Grandma plucked the flower seed with joints-highlighted hands and then aired them on the windowsill. Flowers and seeds, one crop after another, came out. Grandma said, "The reason why the kids enjoy breaking off the flowers is not that they mean to make trouble, but that they were too curious to restrain their desire for some. If the flowers are to be planted in every yard, the kids naturally don't break them off." Grandma talked about it too frequently, so Father became impatient. He said to Mother,

"Look at what your mother has done! How boring!" Hearing that, the younger sister immediately passed it on to Grandma. Hence, Grandma stopped, and took a look at my younger sister and the door of the main room. The main room was shut and the door curtain was softly swaying with wind. The new white door curtain dotted with red flowers, had become pale, flowers fading from red to light purple. Father went out of the room, and then the gate while dusting off his bottom. Grandma gazed after the figure out of the gate, watched the door for a while and then lowered her head to go on plucking the flower seeds.

Flowers, blooming from the front of the yard to the back, produced an enchanting long row full of brilliance. The old flowers unremittingly withered, while new buds plumped, cracked and then squeezed out a stretch of brightness. Holding his hands up, my younger brother was running among the flowers when his laughter sifted and sounded clear and melodious among the buzzes of bees. The flowers fluttered with wind, graceful and charming. In the warm sunshine, the manner varied from flower to flower. Some remained still for long and leisurely, like doing a long dream; some opened their big hearts, as if alluringly messing with bees, which the bees never meant to land on but flew away with a deceptive movement, making the flowers feel lost, frustrated and embarrassed; like kids' carefree looks, some bloomed tenderly against the wind, ignorant of worldly affairs. Seeing the flowers with diverse manners and hearing the buzzes of bees either closer or farther, people produced a kind of sentiment full of happiness and blankness, and attempted a private place for a good cry. Flowers bloomed so ardently and wantonly that people dare not squarely watch them. So many lovely flowers in the soil yard made the desolate yard flourishing.

With a houseful of flowers blooming, people became satisfied and at ease.

Grandma was always on the run and finally tired, so she had to rest against the foot of the wall. Once finding someone, the bees fluttered elsewhere, with the lingering sound durably resounding in the air. The sun was shining fiercely. Although the petals were bedimmed with a thin layer of dust, the brightness of flowers couldn't be masked. The lines on her pale face were unfolding one by one. With the flowers serving as a foil, the senior seemed to get radiant and refreshed.

We played under the flower stems and heard nothing of Grandma for long, so we looked up in search of her. In the burning sun, we dare not open our eyes wide. In doing so, we were greeted with brightness. As if people splashed the clean water all over the yard, the petals bloomed together against people's eyes. The brilliance of flowers might cause the burning pain. Searching along the flower wall, we were surprised to see Grandma sleeping at the foot of the wall, her head leaning against the adobe, a few grey hairs slipping out of the towel and swaying in the breeze, and a small pair of feet stretching in the depth of flower shades. My younger brother also slept, putting his head on Grandma's leg. Several insects restlessly leaped to and fro over their bodies, as if finding no way back home.

Grandma slept in the back of the yard. Father and Mother returned after one-day hard work in the field. My younger sister pulled them there and naughtily let them see Grandma's sleeping looks.

Awaken amazingly, Grandma picked up my younger brother and returned to the house without looking up, her face turning red till the neck. It didn't matter for us to see her embarrassing looks, but the trouble was that Father saw it, too. In Grandma's eyes, it was a big deal. On bumping into Father, she felt uneasy and Father tried to avoid seeing her, too. All of a sudden, a weird atmosphere was penetrating in our family, especially between Grandma and Father. Sometimes, they talked a little with reluctance; sometimes, when there were many people around them, they would not like to say more. Pretty soon, a gap sharpened and what was even worse was that they didn't talk when meeting each other because her presenting flower seeds had gotten us stuck into unexpected trouble.

Grandma stood at the gate, gazing after my elder sister and me. We sent the flowers seed from door to door — one packet per family, carefully wrapped in paper and kept in hand. "Our grandma has some flower seeds for you. The blooming flowers look great. Kids must like them." We just parroted what Grandma had taught us to say. Adults often received the paper packet and praised with smiles. "How cute the two kids are! Please give our thanks to your grandma." Then, we ran home with content and delight.

We could receive a crop of flower seeds every few days and then sent out several packets. Everything was going well as Grandma expected, but she could no longer wait. She, the wife of our grandfather's brother's, was a short woman with a pitted face and beautiful eyes. Before Grandma reached our home, Father had been at odds with the grandfather's and the short grandmother flew into a rage against Father over and over, and several generations of ancestors. As it were, she harbored a deep hatred for Father. However, Grandma got along well with the short grandmother soon after she got to our home, and even was invited to her family. Early before the flower seeds became ripe, the short grandmother asked for some while my parents were out. Grandma promised to prepare a big packet for her.

Grandma's promise never slipped away. She took it so seriously and presented flower seeds from door to door. She intended to do good to all the villagers and especially let kids enjoy various flowers. There were only three or four households left and the short grandmother's turn was coming soon. However, she could no longer wait and asked her daughter to urge on us, "Don't worry. Tell your mum your turn is coming soon." Grandma said kindly, seeing her out in person and offering her a big flower. Afterwards, Grandma limped her way with small feet to the depth of flowers to pluck the flowers seeds. She didn't know that Father chanced to see the daughter with a big flower in the hand at the gate. Father noticed that flower right away, for she was complacently holding it to her breast. Not knowing what Father said to the daughter, we quickly heard a din of a woman's shouting and cursing outside. Mother was astonishingly rushing out when the short grandmother had reached the gate, one hand pulling the daughter and another pointing to our gate. She screamed loudly with anger and wanted the short grandmother's explanation. Grandma popped her own head out from the depth of the flower shrubs, with the pollen and dust all over her face. On seeing her, the short grandmother abruptly became angrier and scolded Grandma, pointing to her stunning and perplexing face. Obviously, Grandma was so terrified that she hurriedly walked towards the gate, with a crying face and trembling legs, saying "Did you scold me?"

"Yes, it is YOU. You never keep your word," the short grandmother screamed on her toes.

We finally had a clue from a din of shouting and cursing.

《赛麦娘的春天》

She said she sent her daughter to our home for flower seeds, but met with refusal. What's worse, she got Father's sharp scolding. So hysterical was the short grandmother that she simply lifted her clothes, patted her buttocks and cried out. The situation got more intense. On top of Grandma's going back on her words, Father seemed to bully such a weak woman.

The short grandmother said, "I would not be Wang Xiuhua if I gave her a break." Kids felt astonished at once, but overloaded with inexplicable excitement. I considered the name of Wang Xiuhua as fragrant as flowers. If it weren't called out in public by the short grandmother, I wouldn't believe that a short woman like her had such a sweet and aromatic name.

I had no idea about when the villagers clustered around the door. They, man or woman, old or young, came over to watch the scene of bustle. That situation helped foster her nerve and she became all the more aggressive. "Huahuazi, come out! Talk with me!" the short grandmother shouted. We were overwhelmed with joy because we got Grandma's name from the mouth of the woman named Wang Xiuhua. You know, it was quite difficult to learn names of the elderly out of the adults' mouths.

Awakened very soon, Grandma moved towards the gate with small paces. Mother failed to bar her way. "Dear sister, could you possibly tell me what made you feel that way? Let's have a nice talk." Grandma said, with the tip of her nose still red.

"Pshaw!" A bite of sputum flew out of the short grandmother's mouth, unexpectedly towards Grandma and breathtakingly upon Grandma's nose. The sputum mixed up with the saliva streamed down at once. Grandma got freaked out, the blood draining from her face. I clearly saw an incredibly big flower quietly blooming on Grandma's face, yellow but a little white. The crystal-clear petals feebly fluttered like bees, and even got broken by the lightest wind. The color of the flower changed little by little, from light to dark, and finally showed a sign of blood-red.

Grandma was pulled into the room by Mother. After she entered the room, the phlegm on the tip of her nose kept watering. Her face turned purple with anger and talked all the time, "What's wrong? How can a woman do that?" It drove her so crazy that she could do nothing but say that. In fact, as was known to all, such a chattering didn't make any difference and never offset the insult she suffered today. Even kids knew that it was a great shame to be spat in public, let alone before all the villagers.

The short grandmother didn't expect that phlegm coincidentally landed upon the tip of the nose and firmly stuck to it. Grandma didn't wipe it off. The short grandmother stopped for a moment, cooled her tongue and left with others' persuasion. Away went the crowd that came over to watch the scene of bustle. Father came in, his face ghastly pale like iron with chill. He didn't look at Grandma, but stared at Mother, and suddenly stamped his foot, saying "It's all the damned flowers' fault. How nosy it is!" Having cast the words that kids didn't understand at all, he left with heavy steps, leaving Grandma in a long daze. Later, I knew from Mother's analysis that the short grandmother meant to make trouble, and Father couldn't fight back because she was advanced in age. Such women of that age were not to be trifled with. We had seen her frightening looks when she made trouble out of nothing. A man couldn't hit or curse for fear that it should lose his face. Worst of all, her several sons had grown up into adults, posing a great threat to Father who had only a brother. Anyhow, this was a hopeless game. We helplessly saw Grandma get scolded and spat. In fact, even the confused could tell that the short grandmother really directed against Father and the dispute with Grandma was nothing but an excuse. This year, Grandma was seventy-nine years old.

  Grandma had lost her passion for flower business since then. She stayed at home all day. In addition to several Islamic worships, she was always chattering alone. The flowers bloomed, withered, and bloomed again. A thick layer of ripe seeds cracked out of the shells and landed at our feet. Grandma didn't pluck them and even refused us, letting them take the course. However, her expression betrayed something wrong. It seemed that her indifference to the flower seeds meant her secret ongoing struggle with something. She heaved a sigh of relief.

The flowers were still in blossom, fervent and bright. However, once carefully observed, the flowers appeared scattered and messy; the branches randomly stretched around, standing in the way; some old stems turned limp, loosely groveling on the ground; the withered and yellowed leaves were piled up, not nice-looking and even somewhat ugly. At this time, Grandma's past hard work explained a lot. We had thought she just hung around among the flowers. Now, it seemed that we were totally wrong. Grandma took pains to prod soil, cut oblique branches and right stems. It was Grandma who kept the flowers blooming in order.

Winter was around the corner. My uncle in Xinjiang came back by train to pick up Grandma, and Grandma left also by train. "What was the train like?" We racked our brains, but got nowhere.

The new spring was approaching very soon. Upon the arrival of spring, Father dug out decayed flower roots and stems, which were cluttered up with the yard so that we could cook dozens of meals with them. We planted almost everything, including maize, Chinese cabbages, carrots, onions, Chinese chives and sunflowers, which could fill the yard up. The sun came out. We asked ourselves in the sunshine — so warm that we couldn't help nodding off. Then, we fell asleep. I dreamed that the seeds we sowed in early spring sprouted and bloomed. What weird flowers!

《赛麦娘的春天》

The sunflowers, corn and Chinese cabbages were in full blossom, colorful and bright. The corn came into white or purple seven-leaf flowers; the sunflowers, erigeron breviscapus scattered row by row; the carrot produced peonies that Grandma had no enough time to raise alive. Oh, this was what the peony actually looked like — as big as a basin. Bestowed with many flowers, our yard was becoming boisterous, brilliant, prosperous and dizzy.

Flowers were blossoming here and there.

Bees were dancing, their wings linked into a sea of happiness.

《生命的节日》
《夏日原野上的追赶》

导 读

关于作者

季栋梁,宁夏同心县人,宁夏回族自治区政府办公厅参事调研员,中国作家协会会员,宁夏作家协会副主席,被誉为宁夏文学界的"新三棵树"之一。发表作品500万余字,出版有长篇小说《上庄记》《锦绣记》《深风景》《海原书》《奔命》《苍声》《野麦垛春好》《胭脂巷》及中短篇小说集《黑夜长于白天》《我与世界的距离》《吼夜》《先人种树》、散文集《和木头说话》《人口手》《左手功名右手美人》《苍山远日暮》等,作品多次被《新华文摘》《小说选刊》《小说月报》《北京文学·中篇小说月报》《中华文学选刊》《中篇小说选刊》等转载,并入选中国小说学会排行榜、中国当代文学最新作品排行榜、《小说选刊》排行榜及多种选本。散文集《和木头说话》、短篇小说《吼夜》分别入围鲁迅文学奖;《上庄记》荣获第十三届精神文明建设"五个一工程"奖,并入选"2014中国好书";短篇小说《小事情》、散文《季栋梁小辑》分获自治区文学艺术一等奖。另获《小说选刊》《北京文学》《北京文学·中篇

《生命的节日》《夏日原野上的追赶》

小说月报》《中国作家》《朔方》等多个奖项。其作品被翻译至欧美国家,并被改编成电影、电视剧。《生命的节日》和《夏日原野上的追赶》分别入选中学语文教材。他的散文总是从生活中的平凡小事写起,语言朴实、真切、纯净,包含着浓郁的地域风情和深厚的文化积淀,展现了行走在世间的形形色色的人们的价值取向与精神追求。

关于作品

《生命的节日》和《夏日原野上的追赶》是两篇被选入中学语文教材的作品,感情真挚、语言朴实、言近旨远、构思巧妙,是让人印象深刻的佳作。《生命的节日》中那个四赴人生"赌场"的"我",背负着父亲的嘱托,屡败屡战,终于用浸透父亲融融亲情的"十元钱"欢庆了"生命的节日","我"与父亲都是在挣扎后失败,在失败中崛起,用奋斗谱写了生命的赞歌。在《夏日原野上的追赶》中,"我"出于口渴,偷了一个西瓜准备"爽意"地狼吞虎咽一番,却被看瓜老爷爷发现,于是展开了一场让"我"终生难忘的原野上的追赶。一个七十出头的看瓜人,还一瘸一拐的,要追上一个十二岁活蹦乱跳的孩子,似乎让人不可思议。然而,故事的结局是这样的:"我"有些疲倦了,终于,我放弃了,但老人并没有把西瓜拎回去,他又一瘸一拐地返回了瓜地。看瓜老人忠于职守、尽职尽责、不畏困难、永不放弃的身影永远铭刻在我们的脑海里。

译 文

A Celebration of Life

Ji Dongliang

July represents a time for carps jumping over the Dragon Gate①.

That July has elapsed. However, it turned out to be a celebration of my life.

For a large number of students, July is of great importance and a crucial life coordinate. It is such a coordinate that makes a big difference in many people's lives. Especially for us, who live in the barren land of Xiji, Haiyuan and Guyuan②, July really rep-

---

① "Carps jumping over the Dragon Gate" literally means "the carp making its way up a waterfall, hoping to become a dragon" or actually "achieving success in the civil service examination in ancient times".

② Xiji is a county under the administration of Guyuan city in Ningxia Hui Autonomous Region. Haiyuan is a county under the administration of Zhongwei city in Ningxia. It originally belonged to Gansu province. It was the site of the 1920 Haiyuan earthquake, which killed at least 200,000 people. Guyuan is a prefecture-level city in Ningxia. This is the site of Mount Sumeru Grottoes, which is among the ten most famous grottoes in China. Xiji, Haiyuan and Guyuan, Xihaigu for short, are poverty-stricken areas and have many residents of the Hui ethnicity.

resents a time for carps jumping over the dragon gate.
I was just like a gambler who bet all money.

  In July, a genuine feeling of being a gambler hit me. I was just like a gambler who bet all money, waiting for a showdown. I found it a painful trial, as if a bud in early puberty was eager for moistening of the sun and rain. I, like a gambler, had lost my shirt more than once in July. What distressed and scared me more was that my father suffered from the same or even more acute painful trial.

The day when the results would be announced came as promised.

  The annual announcement day came as promised. Like many other fathers, my father waked me up early in the morning. Without a single word, he just enveloped me with such sluggish and grave eyes. It seemed to put me in a pool of so sticky juice that I lost my breath. Father seriously fumbled and drew out ten yuan from the pocket close to his chest, and then passed on it to me. He grew numb, with hands slightly quivering. Taking over ten yuan with my father's temperature and sweat scent, I found that my hands quivered more violently. I exerted all my strength to appear confident, only to find my hands trembling more fiercely. Like leaves of late autumn, my whole body even followed suit. I looked away from his eyes, although I knew they were kind, gracious and generous. However, I got stuck in fear such eyes brought. I couldn't afford to lose once again.

I dragged my leaden feet to the school, with inner fears being intensified step by step. Passing by the temple of the village, I couldn't help walking back and forth, and kneeling down before the clay statue. I supposed that no one was more pious than me, and kowtowed more loudly than I did.

The two points I lost caused my failure.

In the first July, the day for "showdown" finally arrived. Handing me ten yuan, Father said, "If you make it, buy ten yuan wine in bulk, but if not, don't waste money." How direct! It was simply because of the two points that I failed to buy wine for my father. I returned with ten yuan that my family was eager to spend. Father didn't blame me for that, making me more distressed inwardly. At the start of the new semester, Father said to me, "Have another try. One year is enough for you to get two points back. Didn't I earn 300 to 500 work points more than others each year when I worked in the production team?" I couldn't make clear the difference between study and labor to Father, and had no choice but to study harder.

I lost again by twelve points in the second July.

I lost again by twelve points in the second July. When I put money before Father, he flied into a rage, roaring, "Damn it! Come back to tend the cow. I have no money to support your schooling." Yeah, in an impoverished place like my hometown,

《生命的节日》《夏日原野上的追赶》

who could deny that attending school meant enjoying life? I wanted to respond to Father, "If attending school is called enjoying life, I would rather bear great sufferings." But such words couldn't be uttered. Father was eager to do everything well all his life. How he wished to cultivate an intellectual to maintain the front show of our family and do something bigger than farm work. He spared no efforts to approve the building permit and finally failed. But someone could get two at a time simply because the son in that family worked as a driver in the county. It was a big blow to those who had their feet firmly landed in the soil. Father fully acknowledged the misery and helplessness of farmers. We brothers didn't live up to Father's expectations, and my two elder brothers went farming one after another, so all hopes were staked on me. However, I was good for nothing. I was looking for ward to the start of a new semester, but still terrified of it. It nev er slowed down because of my inner conflict. At the start of the new semester, Father said, "Go and have another try!" He had no other superfluous words, but every word, like a stone, could make a pit in the ground. He personally sent me to school in the town over forty li away. He walked before me, pulled the donkey and carried my bedroll. His steps appeared kind of tiresome, and even numb. My hunchbacked father seemed to shoulder more and more burdens of life with his back more like a bow. He, over six ty, should have lived in ease and comfort for the rest of his life.

Gazing at Father's figure, I lost the desire for the bet all of a sudden. Why did I continue? Wasn't a better lifetime if I made a change? Didn't my friends and classmates lose their shirts and end up returning? I plucked up my courage, saying, "Father, forget about it. I feel like giving up." Father turned round and stared at me, without any heaviness but fury in his eyes. Like an enraged tiger, he threw his hand and ruthlessly slapped my face with a whip. Later, he went away, speechless. I sensed a burning pain mounting the face, but a relief in the heart. At least, Father vented his anger on me.

I failed for the third time.

In the third July, I, again, failed to live up to my father's expectations. I stayed alone on a mountain ridge for a long time with ten yuan carefully pinched. Later, I made my way into the Supply and Marketing Cooperative for ten-yuan wine. When I saw such crystal-clear liquid with intense scent gurgling into that bottle, tears came to my eyes. Walking back along a path, I, at the age of twenty-two, was filled with heaviness and exhaustion I had never gotten before. On the mountain ridge opposite to the village, I found that in the distance my father just looked like an eagle treading at the gate, with the small-bowled long-stemmed tobacco pipe emitting smoke like a train moving out of tunnels. Father rose to his feet and gave a complete stretch. His body, like a flower that had curled up for a whole spring, blossomed to the fullest. His long arms spread themselves up and down, and made a posture of flying on wings. Father did look like an eagle about to fly away. I believed the bottle in my hand must give off brilliant rays in the afterglow of sunset, which lit up my father's eyes. Father must smell the fragrance of wine representing joy and pleasure.

　　I felt quite uncomfortable being watched to go up and down the slops, my legs seemingly confined. Less than one-li took me more than ten minutes. I was drenched in sweat. While I was approaching the gate, Father yelled in the yard, "Hong Hong, bring cool water to your elder brother. Two bowls, please!" I could no longer help my pent-up pains at the bottom of my heart and then burst into tears. Never did my legs prop up. Bumping into the ground, I said, "I lost again!"

　　Father raised the small-bowled long-stemmed tobacco pipe and just hit the two bottles. Thus, the bottles were smashed to pieces, wine sprinkling all over the ground like moonlight and its strong odor getting around.

　　It happened that my sister came out with a bowl of water in hand. Owing to astonishment, the bowl fell upon the ground, broken.

　　Father turned around and headed for the mountaintop. The setting sun pulled his figure fairly long. I followed him in silence. I had thought that he would turn back to me and beat me with his tobacco pipe once, twice...and even more. That was what I expected. However, Father didn't. Having reached the top, Father packaged it and smoked one after another. Ultimately, he argued that securing an official or championship position arose from the ancestral grave, but never did such a thing happen in ours.

I begged, "Daddy, give me one more chance, please!"

Looking up, Father said nothing but smoking with a fixed gaze at the sky.

As a new term started, Father repeatedly pulled the donkey and carried the bedclothes, sending me to school. I never talked with him on the way, but heard much beyond words. Father walked before me, his back bent more severely, which reminded me of that similarly bent elm suffering from drought at the gate. I couldn't help being in tears until I got to the school.

In the end, I got admitted to a university and my father got drunk.

Later on, I finally bought the wine back with ten yuan. That wine, quite cheap, was held in a black jar and sold with the spoon of one jin or half a jin. Hence, it was called "da" (Chinese pinyin, which means "to buy something in bulk") when people "bought" such kind of wine. Nevertheless, it was true wine, though very cheap. It represented happiness and joy, so it was a festival. It was difficult to get it except on such special occasions as the Spring Festival and wedding ceremonies. As local people said, wine was something that people with extra money could afford. We had no extra money. Local people's money was busier than themselves.

My father got drunk, so did I in a slight way. He pulled my hands and called me "Brother", which reminded me of the scene that he caught the domestic old cow and also called it "Brother". I supposed I was not qualified because he had suffered from a four-year torture with me. If I had made it in the first year, my father might not have gotten drunk like that, or called me "Brother".

Father felt like holding the most splendid banquet in our village. I refused, for I had been a burden on my family for many years. However, my father insisted that it deserve this at all costs, and this was the biggest festival for generations.

After graduation, I could afford decent wine and bought it for Father, but he didn't accept it.

Since I was admitted to a university and then graduated, I had been kept constantly on the move. I was weighed down with getting married, having children, making money, buying a house and handling complex social etiquette, so that I could hardly save extra money for some good wine. Later, I eventually squeezed out some money for superb wine and sent it back to my hometown. However, hearing it cost four hundred yuan per bottle, my father said, "Wine cannot be judged by its value, but the mood can."

I nodded. Father was not well educated, or a philosopher. But his words always kept me ruminating for a good while.

Up to now, that bottle of wine has been cherished in the old cabinet made of jujube wood, for Father considered it boring to savor such good wine alone, and extravagant to entertain guests with it.

Being Chased in the Summer Field

Ji Dongliang

Ever since my schooldays, teachers have written down such an essay title "the most meaningful thing" on the blackboard all the time. "What is the most meaningful thing?" Now, I can recall that all I covered at that time were nothing but good people and good deeds, from an eraser, a pencil, a pen to one jiao, five yuan, a wallet, from helping the disabled and kids cross the street, fetching pails of water and sweeping the floor for homeless seniors to after-midnight lamplight in the teacher's house. Undoubtedly, all of these are of great significance. However, to be precise, they are original, fundamental and ordinary like eating and sleeping. Life consists of many basics, like returning the lost money, helping the disadvantaged or working diligently. It seems to be inaccurate to list them as the most meaningful in our life,

《生命的节日》《夏日原野上的追赶》

which is supposed to exert a lasting influence on us, turn into the shining lighthouse, and even impact our life course and quality.

I have been thinking that the most meaningful in life often remains silent, yet they tend to present their strong importance at a certain moment.

One summer, I tended sheep on a hill. Beneath the hillside was a melon field, where watermelons were playfully staring at me like kids. It was an old man who watched over the melons, his eyes closed and lying under a thatched shack. I headed towards the top for several times, but couldn't help stepping back from the hillside, just like a little mouse attempting to steal grain and oil. I suppose he must have fallen asleep. The summer midday sun dried up the physical strength bit by bit, and even leaves of that old tree with deep roots like being boiled in the boiling-water pot, frizzled up. If he still stayed awake, it would be weird! This sultry noon, for me, nothing was better than grabbing and gobbling a watermelon.

I wandered about, like a fox hanging around the chicken coop in an attempt to steal chickens. The intense sunshine forced the sweet of fully-grown watermelons into my body in dribs and drabs.

Finally, I summoned up all my courage, plunging into the field and picking off a watermelon. At that moment, a yell behind me hastened my pace, with the melon in my arms. Though such a yell scared me a lot, I was filled with confidence when starting to run with the melon in my arms. Providing that a man aged over seventy wanted to catch up with a kid aged twelve, it would be simply a race between the tortoise and the hare. I turned around with a glimpse at the old man. To my surprise, he was a cripple, running like a jumping rabbit. Deep down, I laughed at that old chaser and wondered why he was so stubborn.

The summer field is at its best and green everywhere. The cool breeze is as soft and pleasant as the comb in the mother's hands. I ran on that sort of field like a chased rabbit, and looked back at the old man now and then. He kept chasing with a limp. I ran for a while, stopped to raise the watermelon up towards him, and then ran again. My running on the summer field created a stir. Numerous little animals hidden in the green came out, of which hares, foxes, leopard cats and ground squirrels fled about in wheat fields, while pheasants, sparrows, eagles and doves flied from the grass. Thus, the whole field appeared prosperous and affluent, while the sky vivid and beautiful. I even took a fancy to this kind of running.

A long distance between us convinced me that he must have quit. I stopped to look back, only to find that he kept chasing after me jerkily and unevenly. Hence, I held the watermelon high towards him again, and continued running.

Running without sheltering from the scorching sun was not easy. I was out of breath, my throat dry, hot and bitter, as if I had taken chilies. Sweat all over my body was dripping down like water, my shirt and pants stuck to the body. In the wake of wild running, I fell into a tangle. I couldn't stand it, but he kept it. I could see that he had no intention to give up, as if what he lost was not a watermelon but something else. And it seemed that he was keen on being a chaser on the summer field.

I wondered when he would come to a stop. But one point I knew very well was that he would and must capture me as long as he never gave up.

The melon field had been far away from us. Nevertheless, he went on chasing me as though the shadow that a huge cloud cast hung over me. I couldn't find a way out, as if the horse in the wind, though running faster than the wind, failed to escape from the world of the wind. Fear crept up to me, draining up my strength and courage. I couldn't but give up and then put the watermelon on the roadside. I ran up to the distance, panting with efforts. He compellingly approached me step by step, eventually arrived before the watermelon, and looked up at me and down at the melon. Like a general picking up the enemy's head, he took and checked the melon, put it back where it was, and went away.

The way he departed was kind of a triumph.

It has passed for long, and I've been bustling about these years. But from time to time, I recall my being chased in the summer field, and the never-give-up limping figure of that old man.

《宁夏回族文化图史》(节选)

导 读

关于作者

束锡红,女,博士,教授。1987年毕业于西北大学地理系,2007年毕业于南京师范大学中国古典文献学专业,获博士学位。2001年调入北方民族大学,现任北方民族大学社会学与民族学研究所所长。兼任中国敦煌吐鲁番学会民族语言文字专业委员会副主任委员,河套文化研究会副会长,内蒙古岩画协会副会长。

自1987年以来一直从事民族社会学和海外民族文献研究工作,共发表论文50余篇,其中核心期刊30余篇;参与主编大型文献丛书5套,公开出版专著7部。2007年获首届中国出版政府奖图书提名奖1项,获国家级优秀古籍成果一等奖1项,省级社科优秀成果特等奖1项,省级社科优秀成果二三等奖4项,国家民委优秀科研成果三等奖3项。先后主持5项国家基金项目及4项省部级重点项目,目前主持国家自然科学基金1项、国家社会科学基金1项及国家软科学研究项目1项。2002年度被评选为自治区新世纪学术技术带头人(313工程);2004年被评为国家民委突出贡献专家,同年获自治区第四届五四青年奖章;2005年被评为自治区先进工作者;2007年入选国家百千万人才工程国家级人选;2008年获准享受国务院政府特殊津贴。

关于作品

《宁夏回族文化图史》从宁夏回族地域文化史、回族政治文化史、回族民俗文化史以及具体的宁夏回族建筑文化、服饰文化、器皿文化、节日文化、回族对中华民族文化的贡献等方面全面展示了回族文化的方方面面,以把握数百年来回族人民灵魂起伏的脉动和生命探询的线索。该书于2008年出版,尽最大可能搜集了历史图片,力求完整展示历史原貌;采用艺术和纪实相结合的风格深度采风,灵动鲜活地表现了回族人民当前的生活状况和发展前景。另外,该书突出"图史"的特点,在注重现实审美和宣传价值的同时,浓墨重彩地以"视觉档案"的方式回顾了宁夏回族自治区回族文化50年辉煌的发展历程。该书非常注重视觉享受和美学价值,是一部透视回族历史人文内涵的图文并茂的文化精品。本书所选部分为该书第五篇《黄沙厚土中回族儿女的社会文化》,共计九章,涉及回族人民的日常生活、婚俗和信仰等。

译 文

Part Five
Social Culture of the Hui People Living in the Loess Plateau

    Ningxia is a Hui ethnic community in our country. In particular, the southern mountainous areas are inhabited by relatively more Hui people. The industrious and courageous Hui people have long been laboring hard, living and multiplying on such an old and forceful, desolate and barren land. However, poverty, backwardness and relatively closed environments contribute to the sustainment of their distinctive cultural features and spiritual outlook. Every corner of the land is sending out the full-bodied Hui amorous feelings.

    This is the national spirit of their ceaseless self-improvement, and the embodiment of their total resilience in face of the heaven and the earth.

Xi'an Township in Haiyuan County

    With great enthusiasm and plain shots, let's truly record the actual living conditions of the Hui people in the regions of Xiji, Haiyuan and Guyuan, and firsthand experience the folk customs, religion, politics, economy, culture and other aspects of Hui communities of these regions.

Damaoliang brilliantly embellished with peach blossoms

Chapter 17 Water

Look! The earth lies deserted. However, when the rain comes, it will get excited and then grow.

Water is an eternal topic in the regions of Xiji, Haiyuan and

The locked water cellar

Guyuan. Just like the religious birthplace of their belief, the land beneath their feet, on which they rely for existence, has been lacking water acutely. There is no water source in many places. People here remain dependent on rain to plant their fields as well as run their daily life by accumulating rain and snow that Allah favors. The local people call the facilities for storing rain or snow as "cellar".

"Cellar" is believed to be a glorious invention of the local people. Without it, no one could survive. The so-called "cellar" is dug where the surface runoff passes while it is raining, used to store water like a jar with a small mouth and a big belly and treated inside with seepage-proof materials. Previously, the seepage-proof material is red clay. First of all, people cut numerous holes with the diameter as big as the wrist, and about 3-5 inches deep in the cellar wall. Next, they twist the red clay into the shape of sticks and stuff them into the holes. Finally, people beat the clay left outside into slices with wooden spikes and then connect them. Currently, the cement takes the place. In the new irrigation areas where Guhai? Pumping? Irrigation? Project is conduct ed, people are capable of using the water of the Yellow River while doing farm work. But they still cannot do without water cellars in

《宁夏回族文化图史》(节选)

daily life. In summer, it is required to store water in the cellars for the needs of daily life while irrigating the farmland. It is not unusual that the number of water cellar a family owns can reveal its level of wealth. The ladies, not surprisingly, will never forget to ask how many water cellars they possess when selecting husbands.

Carrying water

The moment it rains, the local people are quite nervous and busy. The urban dwellers hurriedly run back to their houses, while people living here run outward, carrying the shovels for the purpose of opening the waterways into water cellars to save water for future use. There is too little rain, only 200 millimeters per year. Perhaps, missing a rainfall means no water available for next year. In winter, after a heavy fall of snow, it will take on a magnificent scene of the north fea turing pure white all over the sky, the mountains dancing like silver snakes and the highland charging like wax-hued elephants. Nevertheless, the local people have no mind for it. They are engaged in collecting the snow and stuffing it into the cellar for the unexpected needs.

People live a daily life upon the water from the cellar, so do the cattle. In case of water scarcity, the cattle have to drink water

The launching ceremony for the key water-supply project of rural drinking water safety in Xingren in the arid area of middle Ningxia

with high degrees of mineralization. This kind of water tastes so bitter, salty and puckery that the cattle are reluctant to drink it. As a result, people have to play tricks by mixing the wheat bran or rice bran with it so that the cattle can drink it without too much pain. In times of severe water crisis, mankind cannot but drink "bitter water". After that, the ordinary people suffer a lot from abdominal distension and diarrhea. Such kind of water is drawn from the very deep wells, or seeped from the bottom of gullies scoured by water. Due to the serious water loss and soil erosion, such big gullies tend to be found in this area.

In recent years, the People's Government has been intensifying the poverty alleviation, providing materials to make plenty of cement cellars for the public from poverty-stricken areas. At present, the "drinking-water problem" has been relieved. Therefore, the local people always speak highly of the Communist Party when they talk of this matter. Meanwhile, the People's Government has been vigorously promoting the practice of water-saving irrigation

The introduction to film-mulching corn technology into mountainous regions

The impounding reservoir

Irrigating the field with pressurized-water

The increasingly improved desertification control

for the purpose of improving the local production condition and casting off the rain-dependent situation as much as possible. Thereupon, a large number of water cellars have arisen in the field.

In 2006, Ningxia has won over 567 million-yuan investment from the Central Government, and achieved 240 million-yuan market financing and 1.3 billion-yuan paid-in investment in order to thoroughly resolve the problem of water scarcity, making

《宁夏回族文化图史》(节选)

Harvest time

The water-saving agriculture

the construction goal of "581" project successfully achieved. The key project of poverty alleviation and drawing water from the Yellow River has fulfilled its continuously-built and newly-built tasks of 5 pumping stations, including Xiamaguan, Sunjiatan and so on, developed land resources of 83,000 mu and relocated 43,300 immigrants; Shapotou water-control project has been approved by the Ministry of Water Resources and met the standard of the completion approval; East Ningxia water-supply engineering has been completed and put into operation; the first-stage water diversion projects of Taoshan and Dongshanpo have been completed and supplied water; the Liujaigou reservoir in the Taiyangshan water-supply project has been under construction; the Tanglai canal and the main canal of Huihan have been merged and the tunnel of Xixia canal is being constructed; the transition of water right of the water-saving and reforming project of Tanglai canal irrigation area has been built completely and more efforts have been made to do the reconstruction and water-saving reform; both the reinforcement of the Kanggou and Xiezhai reservoirs and the new construction of the Xiaohonggou and Wolongshan reservoirs have picked up their pace; the second-stage input of the Yellow River management project has been increased; the comprehensive utilization project of water resources, including the flood control of western Yinchuan, the Aiyi River, the detention reservoir of Zhenbeipu, the Golden River of Pingluo and Xinghai Lake, have created a pattern of "blocking collectively, managing separately and draining jointly"; the renewal project of water systems in Guyuan City, Jingyuan County and Xiji County has been launched. The government has won over the national debt fund of 153 million yuan and made 225,000 people gain access to safe drinking water, of which 170,000 people from arid areas have bidden farewell to the drinking-water problem. The mission of addressing the drinking-water problem for 200,000 people, assigned by the Autonomous Region early this year, has been fulfilled above the quota. Thus, the government accomplished one of the ten practical things and delivered on the promise. The work finished in 2006 includes: (1). assigning 56 preliminary work plans of the safe drinking water project; (2). examining and approving 60 initial designs of the safe drinking water project; (3). offering 107 million yuan in three installments with the paid-in investment 105 million yuan; (4). building 42 water-supply projects in Wangtuan of Tongxin, Gancheng of Yuanzhou District in Guyuan City and other places; (5). reforming

119 spring water; (6). setting up 30,000 catchment factories; (7). maintaining some pumping wells; (8). realizing the combination of the water from the Yellow River and the local water; (9). achieving the adjustment of reservoirs, dams, ponds, wells and cellars. The government has started to implement three key water-supply projects in eastern Guyuan, Yaoshan of Tongxin and Xingren of Haiyuan and initially formulated —— The Measures for the Construction and Administration of Drinking-Water Safety Projects in Ningxia Rural Areas. Allying itself with Ningxia Development and Reform Commission and Ningxia Health Department, the government conducted the acceptance tests to the second-phase project of overcoming drinking difficulty and the project of lowering fluoride concentration and removing arsenic from drinking water in Guyuan City, Zhongwei City and Shizuishan City. Besides, the symposium on the construction and administration of drinking-water safety projects was held in Guyuan City and all counties were urged to put the administrative regulations into practice.

The new rural construction

The reward of labor

The launching ceremony for the construction of "Ningxia Grand Liupan" eco-economic zone

《宁夏回族文化图史》(节选)

Chapter 18 Farming

Human can only gain what their efforts are devoted to, and such efforts will bear fruits in time.

For ages, the local people have always been working with their faces towards the soil and their backs against the sky. "Two cows' carrying wooden stick" remains the oldest and almost the only agricultural mode of production, by means of which they plow, smooth and harrow the field. Harvesting is no exception. They walk behind pairs of cattle, day after day, and year after year.

The joyful time of growing up

Arduous farming

Specific natural environment results in specific cultivation methods. For lack of rainfall, fertilizer is seldom applied to the soil so that a plot of land takes a year to recover the soil fertility after the continuous cultivation of two or three years. A local saying that you have got thousands of crops and we have got unused land explains this type of cultivation method. Currently, little or no more land has been left idle. Drought causes soil depletion. It is population explosion that makes the soil overburdened.

People strain every nerve to squeeze the fertility of the barren land for the sake of survival.

Harvest joy

《宁夏回族文化图史》(节选)

    Over a decade ago, most of the local peasants bred the cattle which could be used for cultivation or food (The Hui people never eat perissodactyla domestic animals). However, nowadays, they have to breed donkeys, mules and horses in lieu of the cattle. The reason is that their eating pattern differs from that of the cattle. Due to the fact that the cattle pull straw into mouths with tongues, they can eat nothing if running up against short straw. That never happens to donkeys, mules and horses, whose incisors can be used to gnaw the straw, even short ones. The above precisely accounts for the gradual rundown of the local ecological environment.

    "A vast territory, a sparse population but a low yield" is peculiar to the local agricultural cultivation. The yield of per mu land, especially in the mountainous region, which sows 8 or 9 jin of seeds, is 80–90 jin. According to this calculation, one household planting 30–50 mu needs 400–500 jin of seeds. In times of drought, not a single grain is reaped, and even a high price is paid for seeds. Drought prevails here almost every year. The risk of planting crops is even more than that of investing in stocks for the urban people. At harvest time, people pull up the crops by hand, instead of sickles. For lack of rainfall, loose land is seldom hardened and even the sharpest sickles perform poorly, only to pull them up with roots. Therefore, sickles cannot be used to cut off the roots but add much trouble. It is no better than pull them up by hand. In autumn, owing to more rainfall, sickles can be used again during the harvest.

In spite of such constraints as nature, environment, economy, culture and history, the advanced mode of production and the means of production appeared on this infertile land. There will be almost no sign of several or even a dozen pairs of cattle equipped with the stone roller moving in circles and threshing the grain on the ground. Instead, walking tractors and farm tricycles are put into use. (The stone rollers are always following them.) Those who grow watermelons and maize benefit from film planting technology. The stone mill and the stone roller get wiped out from the electric grinder and the electric roller. As a concentration of development for decades in front of you, farm tools with a combination of single -furrow ploughs, rack trucks and walking tractors in Xingren Township, Haiyuan County, reflect the local agricultural productivity as well as the wisdom and ability of the natives.

Nowadays, a variety of agricultural industries for test and demonstration, such as the melon and vegetable industry and the potato industry, have taken shape in Ningxia.

A farmhouse in Jingyuan

1. The Melon and Vegetable Industry

Compared with that in the previous year, in 2006, the total planting area of vegetables, melons and fruits in Ningxia increased by 27.2% to 106,000 hectares, an increase of 29,000 hectares; the total output of vegetables, melons and fruits increased by 27% to 3.039 million tons, an increase of 822,000 tons. The planting area of vegetables (including the melons for cooking) increased by 16.3% to 61,000 hectares, an increase of 10,000 hectares from a year earlier; the total output increased by 16.6% to 2.2 million tons, an increase of 365,000 tons. Of this, in terms of the industry scale, the planting area of greenhouse vegetables reached 15,000 hectares, an increase of 5,000 hectares from a year earlier; the planting area of dehydrated vegetables equaled 7,000 hectares, an increase of 3,000 hectares. The planting area of melons and fruits (including fruit melons) increased by 41.4% to 44,000 hectares, an increase of 18,000 hectares from a year earlier; the output of melons and fruits increased by 54.6% to 838,000 tons, an increase of 457,000 tons. To speak of, the watermelon and muskmelon industry

A bumper harvest of Zhongwei Gobi watermelons

developed at a fast rate. The planting area of Gobi watermelons (the melons grown in the ground covered with selenium-rich rocks) and muskmelons amounted to 33,000 hectares, an increase of 13,000 hectares from a year earlier, the largest growth on record. Under the circumstance of severe drought in 2006, the revenue of watermelons and muskmelons per mu was 528 yuan. This became the main way of farmers' income growth in arid areas in the middle part of Ningxia. The melon and vegetable industry has turned out to be the second agricultural industry after the grain one.

2. The Potato Industry

In terms of the industry scale, supported by science & technology and funding, and driven by the market price, the potato industry has kept breeding of seed potatoes, processing of starch and exporting of fresh potatoes concurrently. The pace of this industry has picked up so remarkably that the cultivated area reached 200,000 hectares, an increase of 53,000 hectares than last year. Thus, it was that year that the area increased most in history. In terms of the quality and benefits of industry development, the system of breeding virus-free seed potatoes has been further improved, and their popularization and application area expanded. Through the promotion method of "four in one, at one go", with an investment of over 10 million yuan for 5 years in a row, more than 41 million grains of potato breeder seeds have been purchased and the planting area of virus-free potatoes outnumbered

100,000 hectares, accounting for 50% of potato sowing area; as a result of the new construction and technological reform, both the production capacity of starch processing enterprises and the quality of products boosted significantly, and export sales of stored fresh potatoes increased remarkably. In 2006, 1.4000 qualified storage caverns were completed, with an added storage capacity of 260,000 tons. From the autumn of 2005 to the spring of 2006, fresh potatoes for export trade totaled over 800,000 tons, forming a situation of industry development driven by both starch processing and export of fresh potatoes.

In terms of the test and demonstration of variety introduction, the achievements were: (1). introducing and breeding 23 kinds of crops, namely, 950 new varieties, and completing 75 groups and 241 sites of regional testing and 40 groups and 67 sites of

The distinctive agricultural undertakings in Xiji County

production testing; (2). completing 46 groups, 488 varieties and 67 sites of various national testing, including rice, wheat, maize, potato and other crops; (3). establishing 10 exhibition sites of rice, wheat, maize, potato and minor grain crops, highlighting newly-authorized varieties and 120 outstanding and promising varieties, setting up the teaching farm of Ningxia University and 2 exhibition parks of minor grain crops in Yuanzhou District, Guyuan City; (4). establishing 14 concentrated demonstration sites of new varieties, with 10 new varieties and a demonstration area of 25,000 mu. Early this year, 22 new varieties have been examined and approved, including 2 wheat ones, 6 rice ones, 7 maize ones, 2 bean ones, 2 alfalfa ones and 2 celery ones. The testing, exhibition and demonstration of new varieties enriched the resources of new crop varieties in Ningxia, speeded up the variety breeding and provided a platform of variety observation and recommendation to peasants and seed enterprises. In order to fulfill the Shandong-Ningxia science & technology cooperation agreement and the other one signed between the People's Government of the Autonomous Region and Northwest Agriculture & Forestry University, 23 new varieties of bred maize and 11 kinds and 121 varieties of minor grain crops were first introduced from Shandong Academy of Agricultural Sciences and tested in Zhongwei, Lingwu and all counties in the mountainous areas. Finally, 6 varieties suitable for planting in Ningxia were preliminarily screened out. The successful implementation of the above cooperative projects added to germplasm resources of crops and provided support for maize production and the industry development of minor grain crops in South Ningxia.

Chapter 19 Learning & Entertaining

You should study hard. The most dignified Allah once taught man to write with pens and what they had no idea of.

Before the establishment of the People's Republic of China, the mountainous areas in South Ningxia had a backward economic development and few schools. Guyuan County (present–day Yuanzhou District, Guyuan City), which once enjoyed a relatively advanced culture, had only hundreds of elementary and secondary schools. Understandably, the situation was getting even worse in other regions. At that time, although people attached great importance to education, few in this area could read as a result of economic constraints. After 1949, especially since China's reform and opening up, the Communist Party and the People's Government had done a lot so that the educational business in the regions of Xiji, Haiyuan and Guyuan developed considerably. However, the accumulated difficulties over time could not be cast off overnight

《宁夏回族文化图史》(节选)

and education remained a stumbling block on the way towards prosperity.

This is one of numerous Hope Schools in the mountainous areas of South Ningxia. A gaily-colored five-starred red flag was fluttering in front of the classroom, on campus, in the village, between the blue sky and the yellow earth. Seven Chinese characters "Guang Ming Bu Wang Gong Chan Dang" (literally, "Don's forget the Communist Party when brilliant prospects fall upon you.") were inscribed on a stone monument standing beneath the flagpole.

The donation ceremony of "Pairing Support" to impoverished students

Nowadays, the enrollment rate of school-aged children is 80% and the dropout rate 10%. Elementary education only for the first three grades can be offered in the village while any other above the fourth grade has to be received in the town. Generally, children board on campus because of a long distance. The same is true with the junior middle school. As for the senior middle school, children must transfer to the county. Of all time there appeared only two university students in Caijiapuzi, one in Guyuan Normal Training College and another in Inner Mongolian

Jiaotong University in Huhhot. Two more had the chance of going to the technical secondary school. According to the party secretary of the village, 80% of the villagers in Caijiapuzi have been out of illiteracy. "Out of illiteracy" equals the elementary level of the fifth grade. Specifically, one is capable of identifying 1000 Chinese characters (repeated characters excluded). In 1995, a formal test was once conducted by the county-level department of culture and education.

A group of children were playing cheerfully on campus. When asked "what gift do you want most?", they replied, "pencil-boxes, bags..."; when asked "what is your dream for the future?", they responded, "the PLA soldiers, doctors, teachers, managers, actors..."; when asked to sing a song, they sang without second thoughts "Oh, kids, carry schoolbags and go to school. Don't be afraid of the burning sun and the heavy rain..." Following the clear metallic sound of striking the ploughs, sixty to seventy children were striding out of ignorance towards their respective ideals.

Few decent traditional athletic sports exist in this area. The arduously discovered and rescued athletic sports such as "wooden ball" and "step tread", once performed in National Games of Minorities, are scarcely seen in the society. The most common traditional sports item is "square chess", in which two players compete. Just drawing a chessboard on the ground, people can

《宁夏回族文化图史》(节选)

play it anytime with stones, soil blocks, grass sticks or sheep dung pellets. In their spare time, players and onlookers are frequently seen at the village entrance, in the field or under the roof. In the quarry yard of Jishan Village, Pengyang County, the chessboards carved on stones are said to be the sole permanent ones in the regions of Xiji, Haiyuan and Guyuan.

As a popular way of entertainment, poker game is often seen here, with the frequently played "Zhengshangyou", "Baifen", "Shuangkou" and the like. It is not only welcome by males, but also by housewives or young girls. Even the females are keener on it.

The basketball game is the most widespread modern sports item. It is quite popularized in the mountainous areas of South Ningxia, especially Tongxin County and Guyuan City. There stand basket courts in many villages. During the slack seasons of farming, youngsters always go in for it for the sake of health and joy. Surely, the basketball courts are by no means compared with those in urban areas. However, the shabby basketball courts can never stop people's interest and enthusiasm

A simple chessboard

·127·

"Two basics" on-the-spot meeting of Ningxia immigration areas

for this sort of activity. For instance, in Mapu Administration Villiage – Nantang Village, Qiying Township, Yuanzhou District, a basketball stand came into being, with two twisted tree trunks and several wrecked planks. Even though without judges, matches were proceeding in full swing.

Starting from the spring of 2006, the State Council decided to carry out the safeguard mechanism reform of rural compulsory education funds. The People's Government of the Autonomous Region timely established a leading group at a provincial level and held the working conference, both aiming at deepening this reform. The new mechanism reform of the Autonomous Region was mapped out as follows: under the circumstance of financial difficulties, this new mechanism, for the benefit of more ordinary people, would be put into effect in all public schools at the stage of compulsory education; incidental charges would be avoided to students in all public schools at the stage of compulsory education (Ningxia is the first discharged of this); textbook grants and living expenses of boarders would be provided for free to students from poverty-stricken families; the security level of public funds for the elementary and secondary schools at the stage of compulsory education should be improved; the long-effect mechanism and security mechanism of schoolhouse maintenance and reconstruction should be strengthened.

Ningxia's fulfilling the project of "Basketball courts cover every village"

When the school year began in the autumn of 2006, a set of teaching materials was provided for free for students from poverty-stricken families. The national policy "two exemptions and one supplement" was expanded to "three exemptions and one supplement", making free compulsory education realized in its true sense. Each party committee and government at the city, county or district level set up leading groups composed of the departments of education, audit, commodity price, discipline inspection and monitoring, and earnestly implemented the new safeguard mechanism of rural compulsory education funds. All education administrative departments and schools extensively publicized the relevant policies of the new mechanism, printing and distributing 970,000 copies of *A Letter to the People of Ningxia Hui Autonomous Region*, providing promotional materials to students and their parents, to reach the maximum number of households and publicize as widely as possible. The central government of China and the Autonomous Region totally invested the mechanism funds of 330 million yuan (of all, free textbooks worth 46.6 million yuan, incidentals subsidies of 190.8 million yuan, public funds subsidies of 35.28 million yuan, living subsidies for boarders of 10 million yuan and the dilapidated house transforming funds of 44 million yuan). Hence, over 980,000 primary and secondary school students reaped the benefits and 537,000 students from poverty-stricken families enjoyed free textbooks and teaching materials. School public expenditures were significantly on the rise, radically ensuring the input into the compulsory education and institutionally guarding against the problem of arbitrary educational charges. Measures for quality-oriented education were improved and the assessment system of students' comprehensive quality established. Various exhibitions related to education achievements, student talent, student comprehensive quality and curriculum reforms were held from place to place, fully displaying the fruitful results of quality-oriented education in the primary and secondary schools. The management of textbooks and teaching materials was strengthened; the relationships among national, local and

A Hui girl from Longde County

school courses were coordinated; the development, selection and use of textbooks were directed and regulated. In addition, the construction for the network center of educational resources was speeded up, further carrying forward the project of "Campus Access to ICT" (Information and Communications Technology).

The launching ceremony of "The Online Party School for Communists" village project in Wuzhong City

Chapter 20 Roads

Mountains were placed over the land for fear that they might shake with the land. Roads of great width were also built among mountains so that they could find ways of earning a living.

It is generally believed that the "road" is a kind of traffic facility. As a matter of fact, the functions of the road are more than that and also involve passing on information. Modern communication devices such as telephones, TVs and the like have trailed off this function of the road. However, such kind of function is of great power in the regions of Xiji, Haiyuan and Guyuan. Just like the most fashionable word "network" frequently lingering on the lips of modern people, the road is indispensable for people to exchange ideas and deliver information.

Located in the ravine of Yaoshan, Leidigou Village in Yuwang Township of Tongxin County, keeps in contact with the outside world only by means of a rugged dirt road. It is narrow,

《宁夏回族文化图史》(节选)

steep and dangerous. Usually, people ride farm tricycles and walking tractors along this road rather cautiously, while any vehicle doesn't work in case of the rainy or snowy weather. The small village, made up of a dozen households, is divided into two by a ravine of over 20 meters deep. People on one side can talk with those on the other side, but if they want to meet face to face, they have to walk so long. It usually takes more than ten minutes even when they make a round trip empty-handed, let alone with a load of goods. In fact, the huge ravine represents the lifeline of the local people because it carries what they eat, wear, use, reap and sell.

The motorcycle is the common means of local transportation. Seldom do women ride motorcycles. By contrast, women in the county very often do so. In the villages, men usually drive motorcycles, taking their wives and roaring down the road. Women's head scarves and gauze kerchiefs waved quite beautifully, forming a splendid landscape. Sometimes, we can see the picture of people carrying bicycles and taking up the pillion seat. It is not because the bicycles don't work but doing so saves efforts. If they travel far, they often "thumb a lift", carrying their bicycles.

Another common vehicle is the walking tractor. If installed with rafters, the walking tractor can hold twenty to thirty people. A large number of people huddle together, going to work or a fair, or visiting their relatives, which appears to be boisterous but dangerous.

The farm tricycle is the most common means of transportation. The farm vehicle with a shed is designed to carry passengers and the business seems to be quite thriving but unsafe. The local people call it "three two eight". "Three" refers to "three wheels"; "two" refers to "two hundred and fifty" ("Er Bai Wu" refers to a foolish person in Chinese, here indicating that the driver is reckless.); "eight" refers to "eighty percent" (80% of people dare to take this vehicle). However, the advantages of being convenient and cheap often blur their eyes, making them ignore whether it is safe or not. Accordingly, the farm tricycle is always packed full, the bicyclers hanging their bicycles at rear-end, and even some youngsters climbing over the shed (It looks like a double-decker bus in the city.) The driver is very tired because he has to work from dawn to night, and tolerate the summer heat and winter cold. If caught in rain or snow, he has to suffer a lot.

Some country roads are hard to walk on, with narrow surfaces, steep slopes and abrupt turns. Besides, the downpour causes many ravines on roads, which seem to be even tougher to walk on. While it is fine, the dust blots out the sky and covers the sun; while it is rainy or snowy, the roads become too slippery and muddy. Therefore, the deepest longing for the local people is to repair a flat road. They have three sayings for "repair the road": first, "push the road", which means "repair the rough road, just pushed by the pushdozer"; second, "pave the road", which means "repair the road with gravel"; third, "asphal the road", which means "repair the road with tarmac". A simple word "repair" is converted into three ones — "push, pave and asphalt". Such three words perfectly display the degree of the to-be-repaired road. Special attention to the word "repair" exactly proves the local people's strong and cordial desire for the road.

Originally, there is no road in the world, but when there are many who have trod on it, a road emerges. The history of roads developed from the trails, country dirt ones and gravel ones into provincial ones, national ones and expressways. In recent years, the central government has speeded up the investment in the infrastructure construction. Hence, more and more roads sprang up and became better with each day passing. It was such roads that connected countless families, villages and towns, and made them into a genuine network. Thus, the splendor from the outside world gradually but resolutely walked along the network into the less civilized world. The slogan "to be rich, build roads first" is frequently found on both sides of the road. There is no doubt that both traffic facilities and new messages turn up if roads come into being. More importantly, where there is a road, there is a new concept and hope.

In the 2006 plan of Ningxia transport infrastructure construction, the investment of Ningxia Hui Autonomous Region totaled 3.51 billion yuan, a year-on-year growth of 3%. The paid-in investment increased by 1.7% to 3.57 billion yuan.

There are 8 key highway construction projects. The Guyuan–Shizi section on Tongxin–Yanchuanzi Expressway completed an investment of 875 million yuan. The continued project, Zhongning–Mengjiawan Expressway, completed an investment of 354 million yuan, in which 38-kilometer Zhongning–Zhongwei section was opened to traffic. The anticipated result that expressways run through all prefecture-level cities in Ningxia was achieved. The continued project, the northern part of rural residence in Erbukeng Village, Gaoshawo Town, Yanchi County in the west of Yinchuan ring expressway, completed an investment of 510 million yuan. Yanchi–Zhongning Expressway, with the overall length of 160.37 km and total investment of 4.3 billion yuan, is expected to complete an investment of 282 million yuan in 2006. Mengjiawan–Yingpanshui Expressway, the reconstruction project of the Machenghe Bridge–Xiaokou Grade II Road on National Road 309, Wuzhong Yellow River Bridge and the Airport Expressway were all listed into the 2006 key highway construction projects. By the end of 2007, numerous construction projects had run smooth and some of them had achieved initial success.

Construction projects of roads at the city entrance and exit: 17 construction projects were scheduled to be launched all year round, with 11 new ones and a paid-in investment of 423 million yuan. Reconstruction projects of national roads, provincial roads and economic main lines: 4 construction projects were scheduled to be launched, with a paid-in investment of 141 million yuan.

Reconstruction projects of county or rural roads: 45 new construction projects were scheduled to be launched, with the construction scale of 745.5 kilometers and a paid-in investment of 500 million yuan. Roads of red tourism sites, highway network reconstructions, welfare-to-work projects at a county and township level and site constructions had completed an investment of 485 million yuan.

Repairing the road

The forest network in the irrigated area

The motorcycle carrying a bicycle

Going to a fair

The view of mountains and roads

New rural residences in Erbukeng Village, Gaoshawo Town, Yanchi County

Building rural roads

Happy children on the way to school

《宁夏回族文化图史》(节选)

Chapter 21 Making a Living

You can go everywhere in search of Allah' favor, but if you often praise Allah, you will achieve success.

The areas of Dingjiaergou, Wudaolingzi, Honggeda and Guzhuangzi in Tongxi County are abundant in fossils of pre-historical life. They are mostly platybelodons, wild boars, deer and other mammals, whose geologic age varies from about 2.5 to 25 million years in the middle of the tertiary period of the Cenozoic. People here have dug and collected these fossils for a long time. Dragon bone, a kind of Chinese traditional medicine, is one type of fossil, whose main function is to stop bleeding. It is said that the dragon bone is one ingredient of Yunnan Baiyao powder, a famous herbal medicine for internal and external bleeding.

During the years of severe drought, people made a living largely by digging the liquorices and catching fa cai (spelt and pronounced similarly to "get rich"). Nowadays, our country has issued the ban of hunting and selling them. Accordingly, more and more people go on to dig dragon bones for the sake of living and it has developed into a larger scale.

Dragon bones are mostly hidden in the sandy stratum under the loess of over ten to dozens of meters thick. It is a tough job to keep digging from the earth's surface to the sandy stratum. Previously, people hunted for dragon bones from the holes which were drilled on the exposed sandy stratum in the water-worn deep ditches. Those holes are horizontal, out of which people take great pains to carry one bag of sand after another. Nowadays, some have done it by means of slant wells drilled on the earth's surface with the old-fashioned windlasses evolved from walking tractors. The means of transportation in the hole has developed from gunnysacks and plastic woven sacks into small trolleys. Those who use the small trolleys are in the minority.

It is a difficult and dangerous job to dig dragon bones. The holes in which people dig them are not deep, usually about two meters, because too deep holes may pose great challenges for air ventilation. People used oil lamps for illumination in the early years, but now rechargeable torches. There is no holder in the hole. In order to prevent the collapse as well as reduce the earthwork volume, the hole cannot be designed spacious, so people have to bow down while walking in the hole. Poor ventilation means less oxygen, which causes people to be out of breath as long as they make extra efforts.

"Fa Cai" (Chinese pinyin), a kind of wild fungus, is black and like hair. As the black one of Ningxia Five Treasures, it is one of local special products. Now that it is highly nutritious and a homophone for "make a fortune", it sells well in Guangdong and serves as an indispensable course in festive banquets. Accordingly, hunting for "fa cai" becomes a traditional subsidiary business for farmers in the regions of Xiji, Haiyuan and Guyuan. In good harvest, they do farm work for adequate food and clothing, and collect them for extra pocket money. Prior to China's ban on selling and collecting them (because such practice causes great damage to vegetation), "fa cai" per kg was worth RMB 300 yuan. In the early years, people hunted for them in the neighborhood. Afterwards, they went farther for them when they found no more in the neighborhood. It took them the whole day to travel with walking tractors towards the nearby places. The distant places were mostly Zhangye, Shanda in the Hexi Corridor of Gansu Province, and Yinshan Mountains in Inner Mongolia.

Owing to the ban, a kind of artificial "fa cai" appeared under the counter. Wang Kailu, a boss engaged in processing this plant, said, "They are made of lichens, fungus, starch and other additives. The cost per kg is about 4.5 yuan, while the retail price per kg is up to 96 yuan. I just run this plant in winter and the annual output amounts to four or five thousand jin. The workers' monthly wage is 400 yuan."In the morning of severe winter, the workers beat bundles of frozen "fa cai", producing the sound of clicks and clacks, on both sides of the road at the plant gate. The artificial ones look quite alike the natural ones, but they taste so different. Besides, their prices vary considerably. It is said that artificial ones can still find their satisfactory markets.

As the yellow treasure, the liquorices are one of Ningxia special products. An elderly man once told us, "As a small kid, I often followed the truck that transported the liquorices, furtively plucking a blade of liquorices and sharing it with my buddies, and such sweet smell made a deep and unforgettable impression on me. At that time, the liquorices seemed to be as thick as our fingers, perfectly straight and releasing slight fragrance, but now we seldom find such ones. It was the predatory collection that led to the severe depletion of Ningxia liquorices. The value of liquorices lies in the root, so people have to dig deep to get it. Thus, piles of yellow sand dug out spread on the grassland, very ugly, like sores on people's heads. Meanwhile, it has an extremely destructive effect on the environmental protection."

These years, Xiji County has developed the deep processing of potatoes and established several starch factories, so potato business turned increasingly thriving. Whenever harvest time comes, vendors collect potatoes in the day, line up in the starch factory in the afternoon and wait for the whole night to sell them.

《宁夏回族文化图史》(节选)

They will return to collect potatoes the next morning. They can only get one truck of potatoes per day. They collect potatoes in the villages at the price of 0.24 yuan per kg and then sell them to the starch factory at the price of 0.28 yuan per kg. The reason why farmers do not sell it directly to starch factories but vendors is that starch factories do not offer cash but IOU. However, vendors sell IOU to those IOU dealers. Accordingly, potato planters, potato dealers and IOU dealers can all find the means of livelihood upon potatoes.

The Hui people are good at business. In the Hui ethnic community, the fairs of Tongxin County, Liwang Town, Qiying Town, Sanying Town and Wangtuan Township are very famous in the southern mountainous areas of Ningxia. On each fair day, people get together from far and near, making the small towns besieged by hordes of people.

In 2006, the People's Government of Ningxia Hui Autonomous Region put 42.59 million yuan into use and fully carried out "the training project of millions of farmers" and "the training project to solve the problem of the rural surplus labor". The government trained 100,000 farmers, exported 770,000 person-times, and realized the service revenue of 3.3 billion yuan and per capita income of over 4000 yuan.

To radically resolve the employment of the junior and senior middle school graduates, help poor farmers out of the misunderstanding of valuing the output and ignoring the training and seeking quick success, and facilitate the shift of rural labor from the physical type to the skill type, the Poverty Alleviation and Development Office of the Autonomous Region began to lay stress on the medium & long-term training and employment program for transfer of rural labor in poverty-stricken areas in 2006. Extensive publicity and mobilization work was carried out by means of broadcasting, TV column programs, delivering publicity materials, posting admission brochures and holding mobilization meetings. The Autonomous Region released the recruitment plan of 5,000 persons and enrolled 5,738 persons. In order to do well on the training work, the Poverty Alleviation and Development Office of the Autonomous Region and relevant local departments tried to find out the real intention and running power of the vocational and technical schools of the whole region taking over medium & long-term training. 12 schools were preferentially chosen to undertake training work and 32 specialties provided. Through three-month to one-year training, it is expected to respectively reach 95% of the passing rate of occupational qualifications and 90% of the employment rate.

《宁夏回族文化图史》(节选)

On the way to work

Tile making

The lime pit established with local resources

Food production

Fa Cai
(Chinese pinyin, Nostoc flagelliforme)

Artificial fa cai

Plucking Chinese wolfberries

Learning technology

The listing of training demonstration base of Poverty Alleviation Office of the State council for the transferring rural labor — the opening ceremony of the 1st training class

《宁夏回族文化图史》(节选)

The opening of training classes for key villages' secretaries of Ningxia poverty alleviation and development

The export of labor service

Chapter 22   Marriage Customs

Unmarried man and women and virtuous servants should tie the knot...

There is a well-known wedding photography studio in Tongxin County, named "Haiyang Wedding Photography Studio". For these two years, taking wedding photos has been in fashion and such a fashion spread out to Tongxin. Many people opt to get married in winter. In the slack season, people have time to get well prepared for it. Besides, food used for wedding reception is easy to preserve. Hence, its business is booming all the more.

As for this, the Hui and Han nationality are different. The girls of Hui nationality tend to be more conservative. They will feel quite uncomfortable wearing too tight and neckline-lowered clothes. Accompanied by seniors, they don't want to feel embarrassed. Although with a strong desire to pursue new fashion, they have to make some concessions. In any case, the fact that taking wedding photos is quite popular in the Hui coommunity explains a lot.

In the regions of Xiji, Haiyuan and Guyuan, the marriage of youngsters is generally settled in several ways: (1) Parents decide. This is a typical type of arranged marriage, which often occurs in remote and backward areas. (2) Parents decide and ask their children for opinions. Basically, this can be called the freedom of marriage and the most common. (The parties involved do not search for their spouses by themselves, but can express refusal.) (3) Youngsters decide. They also solicit parents' opinions and this is the freedom of marriage in a real sense. Now, it is quite common and occurs all the time in developed areas.

The procedure of Ningxia Hui wedding custom is basically like this.

1. Proposal

In general, if a man takes a fancy to a woman, what's the next is to invite a matchmaker to bring up the proposal of marriage to the woman's family. In honor of the man's family, the matchmaker usually presents some gifts (tea, sugar, etc.) and gives an introduction of the man's physical condition, family financial situation and religious beliefs. If the woman's family feels good, they will accept gifts and invite another matchmaker to see the financial situation of the man's family. Thus, two purposes can be achieved: first, to confirm whether the man's condition is true; second, to examine the moral standing of the man and his family. Next, the matchmakers of two sides will arrange for an informal date between the man and the woman, often conducted in the places as fairs, and relatives' or friends' house. If the two sides both agree, the matchmakers will arrange for a formal date. This time, the woman, accompanied by her aunt or sister-in-law, will go to see her future husband and declare her opinion when the man gives cash gift. If she agrees, she will accept it. Parents usually do not impose any pressure on them. It is true that arranged marriages still exist in some remote and backward areas.

In the areas relatively developed in terms of politics, culture and economy, some youngsters find their own true love in daily contact and establish their relationship. However, when it comes to marriage, it is a demand that matchmakers should be invited to give an account of their relations to parents of both sides. It is nothing but a formality.

2. Engagement

Engagement is also called "setting of tea". After the proposal, parents of both sides discuss children's great affair of marriage by means of saying "Salaam". They choose an auspicious day (mostly on Friday, Jumah) and the man's side will visit the woman's side, accompanied by matchmakers, taking some gifts wrapped in red paper such as tea, brown or white sugar, dried longan, walnut kernel, raisin, red dates, sesame, peanut kernel, etc. The man's side also prepares two or three suits of new clothes for unmarried wife. The man and his parents will pay a visit to present all of those to the woman's side, who will warmly entertain them by giving a dinner party. After dinner, both sides will say "Salaam" each other in public, expressing their commitment that they won't change the decision and marry to someone else. Meanwhile, the woman side will give some gifts in return. The marriage, since then, does not change any more.

3. Chahua

"Chahua", literally placing a flower, is also called "accepting bride-price". It means "placing a beautiful flower on a lady's head", showing "the lady has made a marriage commitment". After saying "Salaam", the man's side will give the betrothal presents in response to the requirement of the woman's side, including cash gift, four-season clothes, cosmetics, bracelets, earrings, rings, household appliances, beef, mutton, rice, etc. In Section Four, Chapter Four of the *Quran*, it says, "You should give women cash as an unconditional gift." The purpose for this Islamic requirement is to boost the status of women and provide life security for women. Over time, the religious doctrine has been evolved into a folk custom of the Hui nationality. Therefore, the number of betrothal presents is determined by the financial status of the man's side.

"Chahua" falls upon Jummah. The man's side invites the Imam to give out cash gift, also accompanied by seniors, coupled with clothes, household appliances and jewelry which are purchased in the company of seniors. Undoubtedly, they should prepare such traditional gifts as sheep, sugar and tea. Without them, the marriage would not take effect. The woman's side also invites imams, relatives and friends to welcome guests together, accepting the betrothal presents, frying dough cakes, butchering sheep, holding "Ermaili" (The imams of the two sides recite relevant contents of *the Quran*.) and making a feast.

4. Marriage

The Hui nationality sees Jummah or the even-numbered dates in the lunar calendar as a desirable one. On the eve of the wedding, the bride does big cleansing, named "leaving-mother water", and "Kailian" (shave facial hair with a thread). The next morning, dressed in red and covered by a red gauze kerchief, the bride takes a red bag in which there is a well-wrapped holy book, a mirror and a bundle of "Ai" (a name of grass, namely, "wormwood") mixed with some "Xiang" (spices). They are of profound significance: a holy book represents "belief"; a mirror stands for "intelligence"; "Ai" and "Xiang" equals "Xiang Ai" (love each other devotedly). The valuable stuff must be kept for a life time. The bride is escorted by her sisters or sisters-in-law to the groom's house. The groom and his family wait for the bridal procession at the gate. After the bride gets off, she will be led into the bridal chamber. Guests from the woman's side and escorts from the man's side stand on two sides respectively. The man's side will greet the guests successively, named "Rang Ke". All people will enter the door until the relatives from the woman's side say "well-done".

Visitors can't wait to lift up the head cover of the bride and judge her looks. On the other hand, the wedding ceremony is under way as scheduled. The well-dressed groom devoutly kneels down in the center and the imam is reading "Nikah" (relevant contents of the *Quran*) for the new couple. After that, the groom is about to enter the bridal chamber, but it is not easy. Under the cover of relatives and friends, the groom must rush into the chamber for fear that he should be blocked. The groom's brothers or brothers-in-law may also meet with "play" (The custom of playing tricks on the groom's parents exists in many places). As soon as the groom uncovers the bride's head cover, people waiting impatiently outside will burst into the room and set about the prelude of "disturbing the bridal chamber", but the boisterous moment is the wedding night.

The wedding banquet begins. It boasts its distinctive characteristics, called "Liushui Xi" (a dinner served separately as the guests arrive in succession). The imams are served in the first place (Usually, imams from the man's side are the first to be served, and imams from the woman's side second). They will say "Salaam" before having dinner.

The procedures of a wedding banquet is as follows: (1) serving tea, fruits, dried fruits; (2) serving fried dough cakes, steamed buns, rice and a bowl of chop suey ("Tang Wan") for each person; (3) serving tea, fruits, dried fruits; (4) serving the main courses, with odd-numbered cold dishes and even-numbered hot dishes.

The last one is usually "fish" or "sweet rice" (the eight-treasure rice pudding).

Dinner finished, all people do "Du'a" and then end up in saying "Salaam".

The wedding banquet continues. After the feast, the bride and the guests from the bride's side also go around the relatives' houses, even three to five ones to go on with other dinners. The real sense of such a practice lies in creating a warm atmosphere and knowing relatives.

Although the bride and her husband's mother have known well earlier, a procedure of the bride's formally knowing the mother-in-law is definitely indispensable. The mother-in-law will formally give a present to the daughter-in-law and help pat the dust off (Actually, the bride's clothes remain clean), while repeating the auspicious words:

When kneading dough, do not stick to the basin;

When sweeping floors, do not lift up the dust;

When walking along, do not look around;

When going away, try to be as quick as a gust of breeze;

When standing up, try to be as upright as pine trees;

When washing dishes, do not throw away bowls.

《宁夏回族文化图史》(节选)

Shaving facial hair with a thread

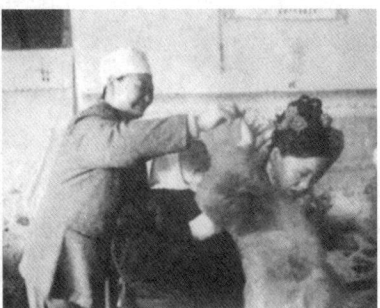

Dressing up

Marriage

The bride's formally knowing her mother-in-law

Serving the dinner

Serving the dried fruits

The Hui marriage custom-Shua Gong Po (Chinese pinyin, playing joyous tricks on the groom's parents)

《宁夏回族文化图史》(节选)

Chapter 23 Women

Whether man or woman, I must make them immersed in happiness and give benefits back to them as long as he or she does good deeds and has beliefs.

Women by their very nature are the same. Women in South China gather by riversides, washing while chatting, and finishing the boring work in the cheer and laughter. Though there is no river, women in the regions of Xiji, Haiyuan and Guyuan feel like getting together. On a sunny day, several neighbors or friends make an appointment to meet up, with the laundry spreading out in the courtyard. The farmyard is enjoying the warm sunshine and boisterous with various sounds — the sound of washing clothes and pouring water, the voice of children's frolic and women's laughter, the ping-pong sound of basins and buckets, dogs' barking, cocks' crowing and cattle's mooing.

Where there is work, there are women. From inside to outside, from the kitchen to the field, from spring plowing to autumn harvesting, women always have their hands full. They do any work that men can or even cannot. In such a man-centered society, it is women who hold it up, silently doing and enduring what they believe they should.

Here is an account of an ordinary Hui woman.

I have no official name but Islamic name "Ashley". I come from Yanghe Township, Longde County. There are many Hui people in my hometown. We mainly live on corn meal. We eat corn steamed buns and potatoes at 11 or 12 o'clock in the morning; we eat rice and potatoes at 7 or 8 o'clock in the evening. There is no meat in our recipe. Unless relatives or other guests call at our houses, we will cook some meat. Surely, it is for the sake of the guests, so we only capture its smell. I have never had meat since I got married four years ago, even during the period of recovering from childbirth. I am twenty-two years old now and I gave birth to two children within four years. My parents-in-law don't live with us. In my house, there is nothing but two children, two cattle, two quilts, two pots, two buckets, two electric kettles, two jars (one is nice and the other is useless), one clock, and one bicycle that doesn't work, lying there useless. What I own are only the sweater I am wearing, two shirts and one coat, nothing extra. My mother's house shares the same condition — extreme poverty. I never had the chance to go to school. So did my younger sister. There is no more farm tool except two sickles, one hoe, two jars and a few baskets. If we need other tools, we have to borrow from my father-in-law, or exchange labor with others. The most valuable are the two cows, 500 yuan for each. Look at the pot! I borrowed the pot cover, no longer used by others. There are only five bowls and four plates. I pierced through my ears, but had no earrings. The two shabby houses will leak when it rains, only to make my family homeless. Two children are enough for me. We have 10-mu land. If we meet with drought, we have no choice but suffer from hunger. My husband has an elder brother. He helped others to fix walls today. My father-in-law is sixty years old and lives on his own.

This is the reality that a woman who has been married for four years went through. The women of Hui nationality are hard-working and kind-hearted but lead such a life. However, they never yield to the reality and strive for better life.

Since the 1980s, female schools have been on the rise in the northwestern part of China and represented the development of traditional Islamic education of the scripture hall. In the regions of Xiji, Haiyuan and Guyuan of Ningxia Hui Autonomous Region, the China's largest Hui community, female mosques, Arabic female schools and family Islamic classes constitute the main body of the local female Islamic education. Women can not only learn much religious knowledge but also improve their literacy levels. In terms of the female school, some consider this social phenomenon as the folk cultural self-consciousness, and others view it as the self-defense of Islamic culture in the face of modern civilization. No matter how the female school is evaluated, there is no doubt that their existence and growth significantly boost the cultural quality and social status of the local Hui women.

A girl's school was set up in the mosque of Malupo Villiage, Liwang Town, Haiyuan County. In this school there were only three girls. Generally speaking, women are not allowed to enter the mosque, but it was an exception here for the three girls. After men's religious service, they had access to the mosque and worshiped, accompanied by the imam.

Ma Chunlan, a teacher in Weizhou Town, Tongxin County, once said, "Our Islam insists on emphasizing female education and establishing female schools, and calls for the equality of men and women. But such equality does not amount to the western civilization demand. Our requirement is to achieve equality in terms of acquiring knowledge, making contributions and serving the people." The female school in Tongxin County not only provides religious courses, but also the courses of Chinese, English, Arabic and math. The teaching staff is relatively sufficient and qualified. For instance, there are a male teacher and a female teacher who has gotten the college bachelor degree. The school-running funds derive from Muslims' "Zakat".

We are Muslims; we believe in Allah; our saint is Mohammed;

《宁夏回族文化图史》(节选)

our sect is Islam; our classic is the *Quran*. Alla is our ultimate pursuit and Mohammed is our supreme model.

The reciting of girl students sounds solemn and respectful.

Playing traditional harps

Purchasing chemical fertilizers

The pilot work symposium on Poverty Alleviation Project of "Lower birthrate equals faster prosperity" in West China

Chapter 24 Funerals

Each human being is destined to death. After a test of misfortune and blessing, you have to return to me.

The funeral of the Hui nationality (The local Hui people call the corpse as "Maiti", and the funeral as "seeing Maiti off") is greatly influenced by Islam, insisting on the fast burial (generally less than three days) and humble encoffining, which means that whether old or young, man or woman, rich or poor, the deceased are all wrapped by plain white cloth after "Wuchang" (which means "pass away", "die" is a taboo for the Hui nationality), to be specific, men by three pieces of cloth, and wearing a prayer cap, and women by five pieces of cloth. They are generally called "Kaffan".

The Hui nationality has the custom of providing support or help in the funeral. No matter whose funeral they come across, or whether they know the deceased or not, they will get involved in it as long as they encounter the funeral. The older and the more prestigious the deceased are, the more people the funeral will attract.

In the funeral of the Hui nationality, nobody wails over and over. In their eyes, death represents the ultimate destination of souls, the disappearance of bodies, the sublimation of spirit and the outreach of life. Women and children are not allowed to attend the funeral.

After "Wuchang", the "Maiti" must be washed and then buried. This process is called "Zhuo shui" or "Wash Maiti". The "water bed" used to wash the "Maiti" is required to remain clean before this religious wash. The imam keeps reciting the *Quran* at the gate, and unauthorized persons are not allowed to enter.

People scatter spices on "Kaffan" used to wrap "Mai Ti". Holding the ceremony of "Zhenazi", the most important part of the Hui funeral ceremony, is the last worship that the living represent the deceased to do to Allah. The Hui general public will strive to lift up the "Maiti", regarded as a kind of beneficence.

The relatives of the deceased wear mourning dresses and some of them are written with the scriptures of the *Quran*. The deceased are put in the grave, with the head facing north and the feet south towards Mecca. The mourners in the funeral recite aloud the scriptures and pray for the deceased to Allah.

The funeral of the Hui nationality is filled with solemn silence. Such occasion is quite impressive and thought-provoking.

Chapter 25 Belief

In the name of the merciful and compassionate Allah,
Praise belongs to Allah, the Lord of the world, the merciful, the compassionate
and the ruler of the Day of Judgment!
Thee we serve and
Thee we ask for aid.

Professionals responsible for the daily religious affairs, are commonly called as "imams", a religious term. Whoever desires and spares no effort can be an imam. An imam has an important social status and plays an irreplaceable role in the Muslim community. About 53.2% of the local people understand Islam, study and accept religious knowledge with the help of the imam, while the rest by means of their family or other sources. Men mainly acquite religious knowledge from an imam, while women mainly from their family.

A mawla is the student who studies religious knowledge in a mosque, and to be a mawla is also an indispensable step to be a future imam. About 17.2% of the local people received this "oratory" education. After "Chuanyi", the graduating ceremony, a mawla can be called the imam. That is to say, he is qualified for preaching—the qualification for presiding over the religious affairs. However, not all imams can preach.

As an imam, he needn't spend all his life in one mosque to preach. As usual, after preaching for 3 to 5 years in a mosque, he will "sanxue" (also called "sanban" which means "dismissing the class compared with preaching") and go back home. Actually, an imam also has to compete for their posts. Every mosque wants to invite an "Erlin", a knowledgeable imam and thus, a rule comes into being. An imam, before being invited, must give trial lectures on "Woerzi" (preaching) evaluated by the "Xuedong" (the board member of the mosque affairs committee). In some religious sect, the phenomenon that imams are appointed by representatives from religious sect does exist. Local people name inviting imams as moving imams, which is regarded as a big event in the village.

There is a village in the southern mountainous area in Ningxia named "Zhangjiashu village" with a history of 60 years. This place used to be an estate of the landlord with the surname of "Zhang" and there was a big tree, so it got the name of "Zhangjiashu Village". Since the reform and opening up (with local people's language, "opening up the sect"), the religious activities can be carried out in public. At that time, the religious workshop in "Zhangjiashu Village" was grand and combined with four natural villages — "Gongjiawan Village", "Wangjiawan Village", "Shanglugou Village" and "Beiyazi Village" to become a bigger religious workshop. There were 1200 religious people. Thus, each year, food for learning of more than 5000 kilos could be collected, among which 6 to 7 mawlas would eat 2000 kilos while imams got 3000 kilos. However, since the joint religious workshop was separated into 5 small religious ones, the income of the imam had become less. Taking Imam Hu Dengshuang in the mosque of "Zhangjiashu Village" for example, his annual food for learning was only 1000 kilos.

It is not a relaxing or pleasant thing for kids to be mawlas and pray in a mosque. Except for those too poor to go to school (A mawla needn't pay at all), the pious Islamic belief formed due to the influence by what one constantly sees and hears is one of the reasons to keep studying in the mosque. They must learn how to read Shahada first "No god only Allah Muhammad angel of the Lord". They will study *the Quran*, *the Hadith* and other Islamic works under the guidance of the imam. They need to pray "Naimazi" (a religious term, meaning "worship") five times a day. Islamic etiquette has a set of strict formulations, from the full or partial ablution, to pray, and there are explicit specifications.

Apart from studying from imams in the mosque, they can also learn from seniors at home, while others learn to do it by means of observation.

The name of the five prayers: Fajr, in Chinese, "dawn prayer", which is about the time before the thorough sunrise; Zuhr, in Chinese, we call it "noon prayer", when the shadow of the sun oblique west until it is about two times as long as the object; Asr, in Chinese, "afternoon prayer", which is at the time between the afternoon and sunset; Maghrib, in Chinese, "sunset prayer", which is about at dusk; Isha, "late night prayer" in Chinese, which is the time from the sunset glow fully disappearing to midnight.

The partial ablution is a necessity before every prayer, which means it has to be performed for five times a day. Besides, a full ablution is required every week. Hence, a "water room" for bath should be provided in a mosque. However, in such a place short of water as the Ningxia southern mountainous area, the water used for bath can always be ensured in the mosque.

People must face to Sanctuary of Kaaba in Mecca when they worship. Because Mecca is located in the west of Ningxia, the Hui Muslims should pray facing to the west.

In fact, only imams, the aged, mawlas, and other pious people will in all cases follow the Islamic doctrine to worship five times per day. The great majority of people may only worship

《宁夏回族文化图史》(节选)

twice each day (morning worship and night worship) for the sake of livelihood, or for other reasons. However, everyone must worship every Friday for "Djumah" (gathering-worship) and on two "Erde" festivals (Festival of Fast-breaking and Feast of the Sacrifice). On these occasions, the mosque is always so crowded with Muslims that some have to worship outside. Accordingly, some people may just as well move to big open spaces in the village for worship.

    Some people cannot attend the religious service, but few people fail to fast. The local Hui people attach much importance to "the month of fast" (September in the Islamic calendar), called "Ramadan" by the Hui people, which is prescribed by Islam. The start-stop date of Ramadan is determined by when the crescent moon shows up. To be specific, it starts at the first sight of the crescent moon, while it stops at the first sight of the crescent moon till next month. The time span is a whole month, starting with "cocks crowing" (before dawn) till "stars sparkling" (after sunset), during which people mustn't have food or drink. The most devout Muslims even do not ingest their saliva, have pills or take injections. The fast means "purifying one's heart, controlling one's desire and dedicating oneself to Almighty Allah". Mohammed, the great prophet, once said, "Fast is half of perseverance, and perseverance half of belief". Hui boys start to fast at twelve and girls at nine. It's required to do five-time worships during Ramadan. Even though one can't do in time, he or she has to do the catch-up worship afterwards. The date of Ramadan always varies in terms of the Gregorian calendar because the Islamic calendar is a single lunar one. The summer in the northwestern part of China is characterized by high temperature and long daytime. Coupled with the heavy farming work of summer harvest and autumn planting, only when people have kind of perseverance can they last more than fifteen hours per day under the circumstance of no eating or drinking.

It is very boisterous at the end of Ramadan, when people get together in mosques to celebrate the Eid al-Fitr and listen to imams' preaching doctrines. The congregation worship to the direction of the Kaaba in Mecca under the guide of imams. They bring their own homemade fried dough sticks and cakes to share with each other. Everyone says, "Salaam" as a greeting, present food to the mosque and give Sadaqah to the poor as "zakat". "Zakat" is a system of helping the poor, also called "poor rate". Islam prescribes that every household should calculate their assets at the end of the year and put the surplus into "Zakat" proportionately except life necessities. The specific rule is to contribute one yuan out of each 40-yuan, one out of 25 camels, one out of 30 cows, one out of 40 sheep, 5%-10% of agricultural products, etc. Those donations can be given to the poor, relief managers, helpless people, and also used for charity work and public service. Such a rule for the Hui nationality is not rigorously fulfilled but based on the voluntary principle.

The Hui people can fully volunteer to fulfill their zakat. On the Festival of Fast-breaking and the Feast of the Sacrifice, a large number of disabled or poverty-stricken people wait for help in mosques. Crowds of children run after adults for "Niyyah". The almsgiver grant plenty of jiao and fen in charity. Although the local financial organizations get well prepared for it when the time comes, small changes are cashed out. After the gathering worship, people will head to the graveyard to recite the scriptures for the departed family. They recite from this grave mound to that one, called "Zoufen (walking along the grave)". This is an important part of festivals for the Hui people.

Another festive holiday is the Feast of the Sacrifice, which is normally held 70 days after the Fast-breaking. The difference between the two festivals lies in the fact that there is a ceremony of butchering after the gathering worship on the Feast of the Sacrifice. Each household butchers one sheep, while several households generally butcher one cow or camel together. At that time, the imams are very busy because each household will invite them to do this butchering. The animals that the Hui people can eat must be butchered by imams or mawlas.

The Feast of the Sacrifice falls into the ceremony scope of Islamic pilgrimage and on the last day of the pilgrimage ceremony, namely December 10th in the Islamic calendar. It is said that Allah created Adam, the ancestor of humankind, in the Arab countries where humankind was multiplied and the number of human beings and materials increased with the passage of time. Later, they gradually scattered far and wide, farther and farther away from the Arab countries. Allah showed mercy on the scattered human who forgot where they had come from. Therefore, it was ordered that the public should make the hajj to the Kaaba, turn their faces to Allah and return to the origin.

Each Muslim is able to apply for the hajj to Mecca, also called "Hanzhi", as long as he or she can feel good physically and financially, and guarantee the safety of the trip. Whoever has been to Mecca for the hajj is respectfully addressed "Hajj". "Hanzhi" and "Hajj" actually share the same meaning, the transliteration of its Arabic one. It is an honorable event for Hui Muslims to make the hajj in their life. "Hajj" is highly revered by the Hui people.

The hajj groups get together in Yinchuan, where they have an intensive study for three days. Afterward, they head for Beijing by train, thence to the holy land——Mecca in Saudi Arabia by plane. On the day when they leave Yinchuan, the square in front of the railway station is crowded with those who see off the hajj groups from every corner of Ningxia, with countless prayer caps dangling in sight. Such spectacular scenes get people's blood pumping. With cordial Islamic carols and reciting of the *Quran*, people cry goodbye to each other.

The Hajj will come back after a month or so, when the railway station is equally loaded with those who meet the Hajj. People rush on like swarms of bees before the train comes to a complete stop, waiting to carry or hug the Hajj with the same wish of sharing Allah's grace. This is truly the same case with the female Hajj.

A great majority of Hui Muslims fail to head for Mecca to complete the hajj on account of financial difficulties. They may not make it in person, but can do with heart. In the distance far away from Mecca, they recite together with Muslims from the whole world, "Allah! I call to come! I call to come! I call to come! Only you are unique. I call to come! We praise because of you. Only you have faith and authority. Only you are unique."

后 记

目前，中国文化服务贸易仍存在较大逆差，文化"走出去"还处于初步探索阶段。宁夏优秀作品的译介工作步伐滞后，对其翻译中遇到的问题也未能引起足够的重视，这将会在某种程度上影响宁夏对外文化交流质量的提高。加强对外交流，重视对外翻译，这是"一带一路"倡议中语言服务的重要内容。

《英译宁夏当代作家作品选》是笔者多年进行翻译学习、实践和研究的一次汇报，也是对宁夏优秀文化精品的一次致敬。笔者从巴斯奈特文化翻译理论的视角出发，尤其对富有浓郁乡土气息、地域特色和民族特点的元素进行了深入解读，对文化信息的翻译策略和具体翻译方法进行有针对性和系统的研究，希望具有一定的借鉴价值和实践意义。

通过翻译实践，笔者感悟如下：对体现民族或地域特色的实物产品和文化现象可以采取异化策略，使用音译和直译的翻译方法，并可适当添加注释，进行文化移植以促进真正意义上的跨文化交流；对有相当难度的语言文化、社会文化、物质文化、生态文化以及宗教文化等信息可以采取归化策略，使用文化替换和意译的翻译方法使译文通顺流畅，为使目的语读者易于理解还可以添加适当的解说。总之，在处理文化信息时，应该坚持异化和归

后　记

化相结合的原则，做到文化传真，促进文化交融和文化传播。

　　本书得以问世，受到了北方民族大学科研项目资金的资助，在此特别感谢院校专家和领导的大力支持。还要感谢本学院和区内外兄弟院校诸多专家提供的咨询和校对支持，以及宁夏人民出版社的赵学佳先生、丁丽萍女士，他们对全书进行了仔细的审校和修改。最后，谨向为本书的出版提供帮助与支持的其他相关人员一并致以衷心的感谢。

吴　坤

于北方民族大学外国语学院

2017 年 12 月 20 日